MURDER REVISED

Sally was still holding the gun, when Isabel walked in.

She saw Terry on the floor. She did not gasp or even change color. She bent over the body and then stood up. "I suppose you had your reasons," she said coolly. "Only—isn't this rather extreme?"

Sally heard her own voice. "But he was going to shoot me. I had to."

Isabel stooped down and picked up the gun. Quite deliberately, she wiped it with her handkerchief.

"No man's worth dying for," she said, "or even going to the pen. He killed himself. How loud can you scream?"

It had been as simple as that. The verdict had been suicide.

MARY ROBERTS RINEHART
ALIBI FOR ISABEL
AND OTHER STORIES

ZEBRA BOOKS
KENSINGTON PUBLISHING CORP.

ZEBRA BOOKS

are published by

Kensington Publishing Corp.
475 Park Avenue South
New York, NY 10016

First Zebra Books printing: September, 1989

Printed in the United States of America

TABLE OF CONTENTS

Once to Every Man

Once to Every Man

It was quite extraordinary. One minute Louise was sitting on the sofa, with the coffee table in front of her, and Chris was standing in front of the fireplace trying to say something. Then all at once the table seemed to be whirling around in circles. She had to wait until it had settled to speak.

"Here's your coffee," she heard herself saying. "Be careful. It's hot."

Chris gave her a queer look.

"Haven't you heard what I've been saying, Lou?"

"I heard it. It was just—"

There was no use telling him about the table. There was no use telling him anything now.

"You want to leave me. That's it, isn't it?"

To show how cool she was she took a sip of her coffee. It was boiling. The end of her tongue felt paralyzed.

"*I* don't want to leave you," Chris said carefully. "It's just happened, that's all. I hate like hell to tell you, but I don't suppose it's a shock. I've tried to carry on, but it — well, it isn't quite honest to go along as we are, is it?"

Her tongue began to hurt. The coffee table was still quiet, but rather blurred. She blinked.

"It isn't quite honest to ask me to be the one to go to Reno, either. You're the one who wants the divorce."

He made an impatient gesture.

"You know damned well I can't leave the business. We're busier than we have been for years. We're making money, even with taxes as they are. And I've told you. I'll provide for you and the boy. You'll not suffer. That's a promise."

She didn't say anything. She wasn't to suffer. She was to cut her life in half, but the amputation was to be painless. Well, for the last few months it had been going on anyhow, a bit cut off here, another bit there.

"You'll be able to keep the apartment," he said. "And of course you'll have Hilda. She wouldn't leave the baby. You can take her to Reno with you," he added handsomely. "It will be a change for her."

Of course this wasn't Chris at all, this tall good-looking young man on the rug, planning for her future without him, planning to marry somebody else, while she was not to suffer. Yet he was right in one way. She had seen it coming. It had been on the way ever since the army had turned him down. He had been restless after that. He had wanted to go out at night, as though he wanted to escape from something. That was how he had met Elinor.

"Look here," he said, "I wouldn't ask you to do

10

this if I thought it would really hurt you. You know that. I'm not a brute. But you'll have Bobby, and that's what matters to you, isn't it?"

She roused herself.

"He's your child too," she said. "What did you expect me to do? Neglect him?"

"I'm not complaining, but you've managed to make him a pretty full time job, haven't you? After all you've had Hilda."

She closed her eyes. Yes, she'd had Hilda. But Hilda couldn't do everything. She cleaned and cooked, but it was Louise who wheeled the baby out to do the buying for the apartment, and who lately had had to worry about ration points and carry home in the heavy pram the day's supplies. It was she, Louise, who did the mending and the thousand and one things which enabled Chris to come home at night to an orderly apartment and a good dinner. And it was Louise who saw that Bobby did not keep him awake at night.

"You really want to marry Elinor?" she asked, still with that sense of unreality.

"That's the general idea."

She lit the wrong end of a cigarette, and the burning pasteboard tip made her cough violently. Chris was looking uncomfortable.

"I'd rather not discuss Elinor," he said. "It isn't her fault, and I don't want you to blame her. She's been damned decent about it."

Decent about what, she wondered. Decent about looking young and fresh in the evenings, after naps and beauty shops? Decent about dancing like a fairy, while Louise's feet dragged with

11

fatigue? Decent about telling Chris how wonderful he was, and how crazy she was about him? Decent about little clandestine lunches, when she sympathized with him about the army, and simply couldn't understand why a tennis elbow kept them from taking him?

It had started, she knew, during the awful time before Bobby arrived. In the early part when they went out for the evening and she would have to leave the table and lose her dinner in the ladies' room, and in the latter months when she had looked like one of the balloons they floated over London. And Chris was fastidious. He didn't want his wife losing her meals in public places. He liked everything neat and tidy. He wanted his socks mended and the buttons on his shirts. And he wanted a wife who could hold her food and had a waistline.

Well, she couldn't blame Elinor for Bobby, or for the fact that he was a strenous child who preferred to sleep in the daytime and stay awake at night. Or that at the age of one year he had a voice like an air-raid siren. The trained nurse had warned her never to pick him up, but what was she to do?

"Hell, let him yell," Chris would say drowsily. "He has to be trained some time."

It had resulted at the end of six months by her moving into the nursery, and now, at the end of a year, with this. She got up. The floor, like the coffee table, was behaving strangely, but her voice remained reliable.

"I suppose we're civilized human beings," she

12

said. "I can take it if you can. I hope it works out all right."

For a minute she thought he was going to kiss her and tell her how well she was behaving. But he did not. Probably he thought it wouldn't be loyal to Elinor. But for a man who was about to pick what she considered a choice bit of poison ivy he did not look particularly happy.

"There was something else, Lou," he said. "I'd like to see the boy, maybe have him in the summers now and then as he gets older. Is that all right?"

"Why not? He's your son."

He seemed relieved. He hadn't had much to do with Bobby, but he had been mildly fond of him. He would come home and go into the nursery, where the baby, bathed and fed and angelic, would stare at him with wide unwinking eyes.

"Hello, buster. How are you tonight? Going to raise hell as usual?"

He was really pleased when one evening the baby gave him a toothless grin. But that was when Bobby was four months old. Now at the end of a year he had half a dozen teeth, an undesirable habit of spitting out food he did not like, and had taken only mildly to housebreaking. He was a baby with character, but he was nobody's angel child. Certainly he was not Chris's.

She roused herself.

"When do you want me to go?" she asked.

"I don't intend to rush you. That's up to you."

"In a week?"

"If that's the way you want it, my dear."

She didn't want it at all, of course. She was still

13

in love with this bungling masculine idiot who was casting her off for a blonde hussy who was merely looking for a soft life with some man, any man, and who was too dumb to know it. What she wanted to do was to take the poker from the fireplace and knock some sense into him. What she really did, of course, was to say good-night and go back and hopefully put Bobby on the chair with the little pot under it. For once he behaved nicely, and she held him a moment in her arms before she put him back in his crib.

That was when, looking down at him tenderly, she decided to abandon him.

When she passed Chris's door to empty the cigarette trays and put out the lights in the living room she saw that he was packing. He was trying to fold the new dinner jacket he had ordered after he had met Elinor, and was making a frightful mess of it. He looked up when he heard her.

"I suppose it's better to make a clean break," he said. "I'll go to the club. That's the usual thing, isn't it?"

"I don't see why," she said calmly. "This is your home. You support it. Why not stay and be comfortable?"

He eyed her suspiciously.

"You really want it that way?"

"Why not?" she said. "It will give me a chance to go over your things before I leave. As I said, I hope we're civilized. Go on in and listen to the radio. I'll put that stuff away. Then if you like we can play some gin rummy."

He looked astounded, but he went. Left alone

14

she felt frightened and rather desperate, but after she had finished she put on the blue negligee she had bought when she had still hoped she could hold him, and won a dollar and a quarter from him. He seemed rather dazed when he paid her.

She had a long talk with Hilda the next morning. Hilda cried a good bit, but she agreed to the plan. Then Louise went out and did a bit of shopping, charging the bills to Chris and bye the prettiest things she could find. She even bought a new coat with a fur collar and a bright red hat, and for the day of her departure she ordered a corsage of green orchids. Paying for them herself, however.

She looked very gay and pretty when Chris came in to say good-buy to her that morning. She was dressed for the train, and he surveyed her glumly.

"You look like a bride," he said. "Who sent you the flowers?"

"Someone I'm fond of," she said pleasantly.

He muttered something about setting forth the funeral baked meats for the marriage feast, and he held the baby, all dressed in cap and coat, for a minute before he let him go. He even shook hands with Hilda, who obviously did not want to shake hands with him or have anything to do with him. But Louise did not let him take them to the train.

"You'd better go to the office," she said. "You'll have to make a lot of money, you know. With two families to keep."

He considered this extremely tactless, even if unpleasantly true, and he did not offer to kiss her good-bye.

"Well, have a good trip, all of you," he said.

15

"You might wire me how the baby stands the train."

He put them in the taxi and slammed the door. He should have felt free, but he had a curious empty feeling instead. But he lunched with Elinor that day, and Elinor was wonderful. She had been looking for an apartment, and she had found one facing the park. The rent was high, but when he saw tears in her big blue eyes he threw caution to the winds.

"Of course, darling," he said. "Anything to make you happy."

He didn't enjoy his food, however. He was doing some simple arithmetic, such as adding up the rent of two apartments, alimony, taxes, and lawyers' fees. When he roused himself it was to hear Elinor mentioning a ring. It was some time before he realized that Elinor was talking about an engagement ring.

"I don't really care," she said, "but everybody asks me about it. I haven't anything to show we are really going to be married, and after all we are engaged, aren't we?"

"Certainly we are. Also I am still married," he said rather drily.

He agreed to the ring however, and he was still doing mathematics on the way back to the office. His secretary eyed him severely when he got there.

"You had a two o'clock appointment," she said. "Mr. Stevenson waited quite a while."

He grunted. Elinor had wanted to make this first free luncheon a party and she had gone right down the menu. Now there was an account lost

16

and probably lost for good. He grunted again.

The rest of the day was pretty bad. He did some more arithmetic on a scratch pad at his desk and then tore it up, so his secretary would not see it. He called Mr. Stevenson, who was distinctly cold. And he telephoned the pressing company to get some clothes of his at the apartment, only to remember there was nobody there.

But in this he was mistaken.

There was somebody there. When he unlocked the door to get his suitcases that evening it was to hear his young son, violently protesting against something or other. He stood quite still, the key in his hand. Then he strode back to the dining room. In his high chair at the table sat Bobby, his mouth full of something he did not like, while a worried Hilda sat beside him, looking a little pale.

"What's the meaning of this?" he demanded. "Why aren't you on the train?"

Hilda gave him a defiant glance.

"She sent us back," she said. "She thought she could manage better alone."

The awful significance of this did not penetrate at once. But he was angry. Very, very angry.

"What the hell did she mean by that?" he shouted. "She hasn't anything to do out there. Nothing but sit tight."

Hilda gave him a look of acute dislike.

"She thought she needed a rest," she said coldly. "She did, too, if you ask me."

He wasn't asking Hilda anything, of course. Louise had played him a dirty trick, but he'd show her he could take it. He went over to the high chair and stooped over his son.

"All right," he said. "We'll manage, old boy, won't we? We'll show her."

It was unfortunate that Bobby that moment decided to get rid of the mouthful of spinach. He sprayed it with neatness and determination over his father's blue suit and new necktie, and it had the effect of an explosion. The resulting situation, involving towels and considerable language, seemed to delight the child.

"Mama," he said noisily. "Mama," and beat on his tray and to the point.

When things were cleaned up Hilda put her case, briefly and to the point.

"I agreed to stay," she said. "I'll do the best I can. But I can't work all day and look after Bobby at night. You'll have to take him."

"I'll take him," he said grimly. "I'll see he behaves, too."

"And I have two evenings a week out. I'll give up my afternoons, but I've got a sister. Her boy's in the war, and she needs comforting."

Well, he could take that too, he thought, still grimly. Take it and like it. He was pretty tired himself. It wouldn't be for long, and he could do some reading. He had fallen behind in his reading since he met Elinor. But Elinor, when he took her out to dinner that night, did not apparently care either to take it or like it. She looked shocked.

"Are you telling me you have the boy? She left him?"

"That's right. Of course there's Hilda."

"Do you mean she's left him with you for

18

good?"

"Certainly not. She's crazy about him."

Elinor considered this. There was nothing soft about her blue eyes, nor even particularly adoring.

"Just remember this, Chris," she said coldly. "I'm not taking over any other woman's—" She started to say brat, but reconsidered it "—any other woman's family."

"I haven't asked you to, my dear."

"Why don't you ship him out to her?"

He smiled faintly.

"He isn't a piece of freight, you know," he said. "He's a nice little kid. Anyhow I don't think Hilda would take him."

The evening, however, was definitely sour. It ended in his agreeing to get her a ring the next day, and—having drunk a bit more than usual—in his having to take a dose of bicarbonate before he went to bed. But Bobby chose that night to put on a considerable act, consisting largely of standing in his crib and shaking the side of it until the windows rattled. He got very little sleep, and he spoke to Hilda about it the next morning.

"You understand," he said mildly, "that I can't work all day and stay up all night."

"Neither can I," said Hilda drily.

"Well, for God's sake!" he said, "get somebody to help you. Get a trained nurse. Get anybody. I need my sleep."

"It's not so easy to get help," Hilda said. "I tried over the telephone all day yesterday. Maybe you can find someone."

He went in to see the baby before he left that

19

morning. Bobby looked bland and cheerful, and not at all like a child who would put on an acrobatic act by night and spray spinach by day. He gave his father a wide grin, and Chris grinned back at him.

"You little devil," he said. "We'll fix you now. I'll pay somebody to keep you in order."

On impulse he leaned down and kissed the top of his son's head. After all this was his boy. Some day he would grow up and they could do things together, like playing golf, or shooting, or going swimming.

"Behave yourself," he said. "If your mother doesn't want you we'll manage, won't we?"

For just that minute he forgot Elinor entirely.

Nevertheless the sense of outrage persisted all day. Grew, indeed, for Hilda had been right. There was no help to be had. Women were taking war jobs, or running elevators and driving cars, or merely living comfortably on more wages than their husbands had ever earned before. There were even no trained nurses. He practically abandoned all attempt to work, and at seven o'clock that night, having forgotten all about Elinor's ring, he called her and said he would have to stay at home that evening.

"Hilda wants to see her sister," he explained. "Why don't you come here? We can play some backgammon."

He did not mention gin rummy. It suggested too many evenings by the fire with Louise. But although Elinor came, looking young and gay and mentioning the ring once, the evening was not a success. It turned out that she did not like games. Instead she turned on the radio.

"This is that new band," she said. "Listen. Why don't we dance?"

She looked very lovely, but he was tired, his nerves for some reason were shot to pieces, and his feet hurt. They had hurt him off and on for months.

"Listen, darling," he said. "We can't dance the rest of our lives, or live in nightclubs. If we can't spend one quiet evening alone—"

He had to shout over the radio, however, and the combination waked the baby. He went at once into one of his best acts, which consisted of getting his head stuck between the rods of his crib, and then telling the world about it. When Chris finally got back to the living room Elinor was cool.

"For heaven's sake," she said. "I thought people trained children these days."

"You can't train a year-old child how to keep from getting caught in his crib."

They danced a little after that, but he was too tired to lift the rug, and Elinor left rather early. She said she had to get her beauty sleep, and of course he told her she did not need it. But the total result was discouraging.

The next few days were practically the same. No help was forthcoming, and Hilda began to look dispirited. She said nothing about a long-distance call from Nevada, however, and of course she did not know of Louise's visit to the lawyer Chris had engaged for her.

Louise had sat in his office, looking very nice

and young in her new clothes and rather firm about the mouth.

"So you want a divorce," said the lawyer, whose name was Smith. "I suppose we can manage it." He smiled drily. "It's been done before, out here."

Louise looked at him. She did not smile.

"No," she said. "I don't want a divorce."

Mr. Smith looked startled. He cleared his throat.

"I see. It's the husband, then. Well, that happens too. I suppose it will be the usual charge, mental cruelty."

"There will be no charge," said Louise, looking him straight in the eye. "I've said I don't want a divorce. I mean exactly that."

Mr. Smith seemed confused.

"But in that case what are you doing here? After all—"

"It's quite simple," Louise said. "He's like a lot of other men just now. He doesn't know where he is. The army didn't want him. He has a tennis elbow, and he's in his thirties. It made him feel as though he was—well, through with things. So he thinks he has fallen in love with another woman."

"I see," said Mr. Smith, thoughtfully. "She's a sort of substitute for the army. Is that it?"

Louise smiled, for the first time. He thought she had a most attractive smile.

"I've left my baby at home," she told him. "She won't like that, but in a way it is the baby who has separated us. Maybe he can bring us together. I don't know. It's a kind of experiment." She smiled again. "I rather imagine," she said, "that he'll think jungle fighting would be easy, after a few days of Bobby."

"Strenous child, eh?"

"He's very like his father," she said demurely.

"I see. And this other woman?"

"She's not domestic. She likes night life. And Chris really doesn't. His stomach isn't very good. He feels awful the next day."

She sat back, and Mr. Smith inspected her again. She wasn't only pretty, he thought. She was smart. Well, good luck to her. He might be out a fee, but what the hell? He cleared his throat again.

"It's an interesting idea," he said. "I'd rather like to know how it turns out. I see the end of a good many stories out here, but I don't often see the beginning of one."

"I'll let you know," she told him as she got up. "That's a promise."

The story, although she did not know it, was not doing so well just then. Not at least for Chris. He was always tired, what with Bobby's nights and Elinor's evenings. Also, what with the ring and an advance on the new apartment his arithmetic was now only a pain in the neck. He was taking buses instead of taxis, and his stomach bothered him quite a lot. Now and then he longed for a good home dinner, but Elinor didn't care for them.

There were a lot of small annoyances, too. The apartment itself had subtly changed, had lost its order and cheerfulness. He needed his socks mended, he needed buttons on his underwear, and the laundry had lost his best shirt. When he went out in the evenings he was no longer a gay and debonair cavalier, but a tired old-young man who dragged his feet when he danced and went home to bicarbonate and Bobby. There were even times when he snapped at Elinor and she snapped back.

"For God's sake, Chris; if that's the way you feel why don't you go home to bed?"

"That's exactly the way I feel. And don't worry. I'm going."

Something was frightfully wrong with love's young dream, but not as wrong as it was to be. For at the end of two weeks Chris went home from the office one night to find the cigarette trays in the living room unemptied, his bed not turned down, his clean pajamas not home from the laundry, and a fully dressed Hilda waiting for him in the hall with Bobby in her arms.

"I've got to leave," she said. "My sister's sick. She hasn't heard from her boy, and she's sick. She's sent for me."

He stared at her, speechless.

"But you can't," he managed to say. "You can't leave me like this. What on earth will I do?"

"I'm afraid that's up to you," said Hilda. "After all it needn't have happened. You had a good wife, and a pretty one. If you wanted to get rid of her for that—that blondined creature you brought in here, that's your business. It's not mine."

To his horror she handed him the boy and picked up a suitcase.

"I've left his diet list in the kitchen, along with the ration books," she said listlessly. "And don't forget to put him on his chair, will you? He's always been regular."

She kissed the baby, and without another word

went out the door. Although she closed it quietly it sounded like the crack of doom to him. He was alone, he and his son. There was nobody now, nobody to cook a meal or wash the dishes. Nobody even to send out for food. He stood there helplessly, the child in his arms.

He opened a can of salmon for his dinner that night, and he managed to bathe Bobby without drowning him. Not without a close escape, however. He went to look for a towel, and the child was submerged when he got back. Chris broke into a cold sweat, but the baby's lungs were all right. Were wonderful, in fact. They both slept very well that night, probably due to exhaustion, and as Hilda had left some cooked cereal he managed breakfast for Bobby. That is, he got some of it into his son. The remainder, depending on whether Bobby chose to swallow it or not, landed like the wind, whither it listed.

There was no question of going to the office, of course. He spent most of the day at the telephone trying to get help, and naturally he forgot the baby's chair. The results were disastrous in both cases, and at five that afternoon he faced his situation. He had missed two important business conferences, there was nothing to eat in the house, his bed had been made by the simple method of drawing up the covers, he himself was still in pajamas and dressing gown, and the baby after a hard-boiled egg for lunch was yelling his head off. In desperation he opened a can of baked beans, and was feeding them to him when Elinor called up. He answered the phone with his son in his lap, tugging at the cord, and with the beans hither and yon on his pajamas.

"Hello, big boy," said Elinor gaily. "What's on for tonight? I've heard of a new place. How about trying it?"

He tried to control his voice.

"I'm afraid there's nothing doing," he said. "Hilda has walked out on me. I'm alone here."

"Why, you poor darling!" said Elinor, still cheerfully. "You'll have to get somebody else, won't you?"

"Try it and see!" He gritted his teeth, and released the cord from around Bobby's neck, where it was slowly choking him to death. "Look, Elinor, this is no joke. I'm in a jam and I need help. Why don't you come over? And while you're doing it you might bring a steak. I'm starving."

"A steak!" she said incredulously. "Are you asking me to come over there and *cook* for you? I don't know how to cook."

"You needn't cook it," he said patiently. "I'll try my hand at it. All you have to do is to look after the baby while I do it."

Her voice was distinctly cold.

"Listen, Chris," she said. "I don't know anything about babies. It does seem to me that you've managed everything badly. Anyhow I've got a terrible headache. I'd just as soon rest tonight. Maybe I can telephone around and get somebody for you."

"Don't bother," he said. "Don't give it another thought. I can manage."

He was possessed of a furious rage as he put

down the receiver. Elinor didn't have a headache. She had no head to ache. She had no heart, either. All she had was a pretty face and body, and a pair of tireless feet. He looked down at his son, now sleeping on his knee, and around at the apartment, which looked as though a minor tornado had passed through it. Then he felt his unshaven face, and after that he put Bobby in his crib and going back to the pantry opened another can of salmon, sitting on the edge of the kitchen table to eat it.

The next morning he telephoned his office that he was down with the flu, and at ten o'clock he rather sketchily dressed his son, who had breakfasted on a fried egg this time, and put him into his perambulator. The elevator man eyed him curiously as they started for the street.

"It's a long time since I seen a man wheel a baby carriage," he said. "In this neighborhood anyhow."

"Well, you're seeing it now," said Chris coldly.

"Kinda nice kid you got there."

"He's all right," said Chris. "Only he has to eat."

"What you been feeding him?"

"Fried eggs and baked beans," said Chris, and headed for the street.

A good many people grinned when they saw him, but he shut his jaw firmly. This was his child, and by God, whether his mother had abandoned him or not, he wasn't going to let him starve. Halfway to the grocer's, however, he remembered the ration books. He had to turn and go back for them, and for the first time he realized how heavy and hard to manage was an English perambulator.

Maybe life hadn't been so simple for Lou, after

27

all. Take this matter of food, for instance, and all this nonsense about ration points. Take this pram, and Bobby night as well as day, wheeling him to the park, feeding him, bathing him, dressing him, even the chair business. No wonder she was tired sometimes. He himself was exhausted.

He felt an acute nostalgia for the old days, for their quiet evenings, for his mended socks and his ordered home, for gin rummy and an occasional beefsteak and a chance to attend to his job without a hangover. And those orchids when she started for Reno. Who was sending her orchids?

He got the ration books and started out again. The pram by that time was approximately the weight of a jeep, and when he finally reached the grocer's he found that buying was not the simple thing it had appeared. He could, on his points, have steak or butter, but not both. To his surprise too he found that he was expected to carry his purchases home. As he had bought lavishly this meant practically submerging Bobby, who protested at the top of his lungs, and was finally soothed only with — at the grocer's suggestion — a pickled pig's knuckle.

"Gives 'em something to chew on," he said. "My kids love 'em."

Chris was sweating when he got back to the apartment. He wheeled the pram, now approximately the weight of a tank, into the hall and stopped for breath.

To his amazement he heard someone moving about in the kitchen.

"That you, Hilda?" he called hopefully.

When there was no answer he glanced into the living room. The windows were up, and it looked its former tidy self. Beyond it the breakfast dishes had been moved from the dining room, and suddenly he realized that from the kitchen was coming the odor of something frying, and the aroma of good strong coffee.

He was still standing there when Louise stepped out into the hall. She wore her hat, but her sleeves were rolled up, and the odor of good cooking was all around her, like an aura. He gave her a sickly smile, but she did not smile back. She walked firmly to the carriage, removed the pig's knuckle, and then looked at him coldly.

"I suppose living this way is your idea of love's young dream," she said. "I must say it's pretty dirty."

He tried to summon an air of dignity.

"What did you expect?" he said. "Hilda had to go to her sister."

"I know all that," she said impatiently. "She wired me and I flew back. Where's Elinor?"

"I don't know. What's more I don't care."

But Louise did not melt.

"So she wouldn't take the job," she said. "I didn't think she would." She looked down at Bobby, still buried in his pram and fishing for the pig's knuckle. "What have you been feeding him?" she inquired.

"Well, look at him," Chris said defensively. "He looks all right, doesn't he? We managed. We got along fine."

"What have you fed him?"

"Milk and cereal."

"What else?"

"He's had some canned salmon, and some baked beans." She looked startled, but he went on. "Now see here," he said, "don't act so darned superior. We like each other. We don't want women butting in, telling us what to do."

She was still cold, however.

"Some woman should have suggested that at least you could shave."

"Shave?" he said bitterly. "With a baby under my arm?"

"That's the way I usually do my hair."

Suddenly he felt exhausted. He sat down on a hall chair.

"What's been going on here?" he demanded. "Why didn't you tell me how heavy that carriage was? And that you were bringing home the groceries?"

"I didn't think you were interested."

"Well, that's over, if it's any good to you."

"That remains to be seen," she said, still in that crisp new voice of hers. "At least you can eat. I brought some pork chops. Now if you'll disinter your son I'll wash him. He looks as though he needs it."

Here, however, something unexpected happened. When she picked up Bobby he eyed her distrustfully, let out a whoop and held out his arms to his father.

"Dada," he said distinctly.

"Give him to me," said Chris, in a masterful voice. "He and I understand each other, don't we, son?" He took him and the baby gave him a beatific grin. "That's right, boy. Show her she isn't so damned important after all."

Her eyes were soft as she looked at them, the messy baby, the tired unshaven man who had tried to divorce her. But she was careful not to let him see them.

"You'd better shave and then call the office," she said. "I'll give you your lunch when it's ready."

He looked at her. She had not forgiven him. She had come back for the emergency, but that was all. And somewhere in the offing was this unknown who sent her orchids. Well, he deserved what he'd got. He went drearily into the bathroom and got out his razor.

He returned from the office that evening to find Bobby asleep and the apartment fresh and clean. There were flowers and candles on the table, and when Louise called him to dinner there was a thick broiled steak. But his appetite had gone back on him. He could only stare across the table at the detached and charming woman he had tried to get rid of.

"I've been an awful fool, Lou," he said. "I suppose I don't need to tell you that."

"No, you don't need to tell me," she said drily. "I ought to know."

But it was not until she was behind the coffee table, pouring out coffee, that she let him talk. And this time it was Chris who burned his tongue. He could still talk, however. He verbally got down on his knees while he told her his troubles, and the table did not whirl at all.

31

"What you are telling me," she said, "is that you want a housekeeper and a nurse. That's it, isn't it?"

"You sound like Elinor," he said bitterly. "No, I don't. I want you back, as a wife. If you don't care about me you might at least think of Bobby."

"I suppose Elinor is out?"

"She was never really in, Lou."

She sat very still. Perhaps he thought that was true. Perhaps at least once to every man there came a time when life seemed dull and settled, and he had somehow to renew his youth. That was the time for the wife to use her head. She hoped she had used hers.

Apparently she had, for Chris was coming toward her and the coffee table was threatening to whirl again.

Late that night with both Bobby and Chris asleep, she went stealthily to the telephone in the living room and called a number. As she waited she looked about the dear familiar room, its ash trays emptied, its cushions smooth, and the poker with which she had once longed to knock some sense into her husband still a merely useful utensil for poking the fire. She felt calm and happy. When a drowsy voice finally answered her her voice was almost gay.

"It's all right, Hilda," she said. "It worked wonderfully. You can come back in the morning."

The Fishing Fool

The Fishing Fool

I was giving one of the waitresses a permanent wave the night it happened. It was about one o'clock in the morning and I had just finished wrapping her, Minnie being the sort of girl who wants fifty curls for five dollars, and she didn't get down from the hotel dining room until almost eleven.

Right away when she came in I saw something had happened.

"They've had a quarrel or something, Ethel," she said. "He's eating at his own table tonight, and he looks fit to be tied."

"Maybe he's got some sense at last," I said bitterly. "He only had ten days, and for seven of them he's been firing golf balls into the Gulf of Mexico instead of fishing."

"That's love, I guess," said Minnie.

"That's poppycock," I said sharply. "Now he's lost Joe, the best fish guide on the island. He hasn't even a boat. And the tarpon are in."

I was pretty sore. For years, ever since he used to

come from college on Easter vacation, Win McKnight and Joe had kept up the reputation of the island for tarpon against all the other resorts around. Almost always he got the first fish, and almost always the biggest. He'd had five gold-button fish in the last five years, which means that each weighed over a hundred pounds, and all of us felt that the season hadn't really commenced until he got there. Now he had only ten days' leave before he went into the army, and for an entire week, instead of being out in the Pass for the big fellows, he had been trailing a girl around the golf course. And making a fool of himself doing it.

I shoved Minnie over the basin for the shampoo to shut her up, but she came up still talking.

"It's funny, isn't it, Ethel," she said. "That she won't fish, I mean."

"Maybe her mother was scared by a fish before she was born."

Minnie giggled but I was still sore. The hotel stands on a slope, and my shop is in the basement at the rear. From my windows I can see the guide dock, and I knew that every boat on the island was in the Pass that night, ready to fish the slack tide at two A.M. Even Joe was there. But not Mack. Win McKnight was always Mack to us. No, not Mack. He was upstairs in bed. Not sleeping. I didn't think he was asleep. But letting us down when we needed the business, and that because he'd fallen for a girl who probably thought one went after tarpon with a worm for bait, and just didn't give a damn anyhow.

Not that Mack meant anything to me personally. At forty-five and a hundred and sixty pounds a woman quits fooling herself. But I'd always liked him. He'd stick his head in my door on his way down to the guide dock and grin at me.

"How's the beauty business, Ethel?"

"Rotten. What's the use? You men never look at anything but fish."

As I say, I liked him, which made it worse. When I had appendicitis it had been Mack — and Joe — who wrapped me in a blanket, carried me to the boat and got me to the hospital on the mainland before the abscess ruptured. He paid my bills, too. After that he could have used me for tarpon bait if he'd wanted to, and when I heard he was going into the army from the National Guard I took the newspaper down to Joe, and we both looked pretty sick.

"He's a good guy," Joe said. "Best man with a fish I ever saw."

Only tarpon are fish on the island. The other little fellows have names.

Naturally then there was considerable excitement when we learned he was coming. His wire said: "Have ten days before showing army how to fight. Wake Joe from his winter sleep. Also notify fish."

It meant a lot, because the season had been bad; late and cold, with now and then a tarpon rolling but none taken. You see, Mack was a sort of legend by that time. And when he did arrive about half the hotel met him on the dock. I myself was there. We let out a cheer when we saw him, and he grinned and waved. But the cheer sort of died away when we saw that he wasn't alone. There was a girl behind him, and the way he helped her off the boat showed me right away how things stood.

"Well, here we are, Miss Jeffries," he said. "Welcome to Corella Island."

She looked around her, at us and at the island; at the cocoanut palms and the orange trees and the blooming hibiscus and the long stretches of white sandy beach. It is beautiful, if I do say it. But I thought she looked rather queer.

"It's lovely," she said. "But it *does* smell fishy, doesn't it?"

"Sure it does," he said happily. "And how!"

I caught Joe's eye as the bellboys were taking off their stuff. Mack had his usual leather rod-case and tackle-box, but the Jeffries girl had a bag of golf clubs. Joe looked at them, and I could tell pretty well how he felt. You see, we get two sorts of guests, the fishing crowd and the golf crowd, and the split between would make the Grand Canyon look like a drainage ditch. He took the tackle after Mack had shaken hands with him.

"Good tide tonight, Mack," he said. "Slack water at half-past ten."

But Mack looked undecided.

"I'll let you know, Joe. I've had a long trip."

Right then and there I knew it was all over. So did Joe. And if you'll believe me, it was. They had met on the train, the Jeffries girl and Mack, and I gathered that the only time he'd taken his eyes off her since was when he was asleep.

She was worth looking at, at that. I see all sorts of girls in my business, but Peggy Jeffries was about tops; one of those natural blondes who don't need a sunshine rinse, and so slim that I went off bread and potatoes that very night at dinner.

By that time, of course, everybody knew something was wrong. Usually when Mack arrives he is in fishing clothes as soon as he can unpack them, and in the Pass as soon as he can get there. But that evening he put on white flannels and a snappy sports coat, and if you'll believe me he and the Jeffries girl played backgammon until bedtime. I don't think he knew what he was playing. I slipped up the stairs once to put a quarter in one of the slot machines and Slim, the bartender, came to the door and winked at me.

"What will you bet she lands him?" he said. "He isn't even jumping to throw the hook."

"Maybe he's tired."

"Maybe I don't know a bottle of Scotch when I see it."

The worst news came the next morning. When Bill, the golf pro, came to lunch in the staff dining room he said he had bought a set of clubs and was taking lessons, with the girl looking on.

"How is he?" I asked, my heart sinking.

"Terrible," he said. "I left the caddies in bathing trunks, hunting for the six new balls he drove into the water."

Well, that's the way it was, day after day. Joe sitting in his boat waiting, with nothing to do; nobody catching any fish, and Mack on the links, with his face grim and the girl insisting on making a golfer of him if it killed him.

39

I saw him myself one morning when I was taking a walk before I started work. He was twisted up like a pretzel, and he was in a bad temper, too. The girl was standing by, watching him anxiously.

"Look, Mack," she said. He was Mack to her by that time, of course, and she was Peggy. "You don't have to kill it. It isn't Hitler. It's just a plain little white ball, waiting to be smacked."

"I'll smack it all right," he said furiously.

He hauled off and hit at it, and it should have gone three hundred yards. It only rolled about thirty feet however, and he looked as if he couldn't believe it. Then he turned and gave her a funny sort of smile.

"Look," he said. "I can do a few things. I can ride a horse. I can play tennis. I can shoot a gun. I can even fish. Then why the eternal hell can't I hit that ball?"

"You'll get it, Mack. It only needs practice."

She teed her ball and sent it clear down the fairway to the edge of the green. She waited until it stopped rolling, and then looked at him. Not patronizing. Not even proud of the shot. She really was a nice girl, only she didn't understand a man like Mack. Or that any man hates to have a girl make him look like a fool.

"Of course I've played for years," she said apologetically.

But he didn't reply. He stood looking off at the ball. Then he dropped his club.

"Oh God!" he said, and left her standing there.

I had a bit of hope then, but the next day she had him back. The plain truth was that, as Slim said, the poor lug was so in love with her that he couldn't keep away from her. And she hadn't the faintest idea what she was doing to him. She looked frightfully happy. She never noticed that he was avoiding the other guests. But she simply refused to get in a boat, and he wouldn't go without her.

Everybody on the island was watching, of course. The water was warming up, and here were the tarpon coming in—or showing up. Because there is an endless argument about them among the guides, one side believing they are in the Pass all year, but only showing in the spring; the other insisting that they spend the cold weather somewhere out in the Gulf, watching the thermometer until it's well toward seventy before they move. And here was our last hope playing the infatuated fool: golf and a swim in the morning, a sunbath in the afternoon, bridge or backgammon at night. And the Pass full of boats from everywhere around, waiting to take our record away from us.

I saw Joe alone at the guide dock one afternoon. All the rest were gone, and he was fishing for pinfish with a speck of shrimp and a hook about the size of my little fingernail. As I watched him he got one about five inches long. He put it carefully in the fish well. Then he looked at me.

"Can that girl swim, Ethel?" he inquired.

"Like a duck," I said. "Why?"

He drew a long breath. "I was thinking of taking her somewhere and drowning her."

He caught another pinfish and looked at it with anguish. "Look. That's bait if I ever saw it. I'm loaded with bait. Them fish is going to strike any day."

"Maybe I can work on her," I told him. "I don't think she really understands, Joe."

"You work on her and see where it gets you!"

I had a try, at that. She came down that afternoon for a manicure, and I told her she had good hands for fishing, strong enough even for tarpon. She just smiled.

"It's funny," she said. "So many people here want me to fish. It's silly, isn't it? I can't see why any man thinks it's sport to pull some helpless little thing out of the water and gasp itself to death."

"There's nothing little or helpless about a tarpon, Miss Jeffries."

"They kill them, don't they?"

"Only the first one, or something extra special. They let the others go."

I tried to tell her about it. How when the tarpon really come in and you see them, you never forget it; how they come up and roll, and it's your guess whether they weigh fifty pounds or a hundred and fifty. How when you strike one you think you're going out of the boat after it, and how it leaps into the air and shakes its head, and the chances are two to one that it will throw the hook and depart for parts unknown.

But I saw it was no use. She just wasn't interested. However she gave me a dollar tip, which is unusual, and I had Slim in the bar change it into quarters and took them to the slot machine. I got a lemon every time, and Slim grinned at me from the door of the bar.

"Why don't you break the glass?" he said. "That's the only way you'll get anything out of it."

I went in to the bar and got a coke. Slim's an old friend of mine.

"I wish you'd tell me something, Slim," I said. "What sort of fellow lets a girl make a doormat of him, with welcome on it?"

"Every fellow, once in a lifetime. Why don't you let that machine alone?"

"I'm trying to get my train fare back home."

"You might try saving it, just for a change," he said. "I suppose Mack's the doormat?"

"He is."

"Give him time. It took a stiff Scotch to get him to that backgammon board last night. And the girl's all right. Just needs experience. You watch. He'll break her neck some day and she'll like it."

"I'd like it myself," I said.

The truth was we were all pretty much on edge by that time. The fishing crowd was talking about going North, which meant closing the hotel. So every one was grumpy, including the guides, and one day someone put an anonymous sign on the bulletin board.

"When will Mack break the hoodoo?"

He tore it down when he saw it, but the next morning things began to happen.

The tarpon showed up. All at once word came that the Pass was full of them, and I knew what that meant. The hotel simply seethed that day. At the guide dock the bait man was doing a big business in pinfish, crabs and dried mullet. The

43

tackle stand was selling reels and fresh lines, and about noon I met Joe, loaded down with lunch boxes, on the way to his boat. I don't know when I've been so excited.

"Bring me back a big one, Joe," I said.

He stopped and looked at me.

"What sort?" he inquired. "Angel wings or conch?"

"Are you being funny?"

"Funny!" he snarled. "The fish are in. The place is full of them. So we're going to lunch somewhere on a beach and then gather shells. I've been in this business thirty years. I've guided for Mack for five. I got him the only diamond-button fish on this island since Wilson was President. So I'm going shelling."

He dropped one of the lunch boxes and deliberately put his foot on it.

"Maybe them hard-boiled eggshells won't be so good when she gets them," he said.

I wanted to howl my head off.

I watched them start that day, and if ever a man had a hangdog look Mack had. But she still hadn't an idea what she was doing. She saw me at my window and waved, but to save my soul I couldn't wave back. I went up and put a quarter in the slot machine, just to work off steam. I got two dollars out, but like a fool I played them back for the jackpot and lost them all.

Mind you, I don't think Mack let go without a struggle. He had even coaxed her to troll a line on the way across the bay to the shell beach. According to Joe she got a sea trout, and a big one. But she wouldn't look at it. She made Joe put it back in the water, which hurt since trout were scarce and it would have made Joe and some of the other guides a supper.

So I think nobody was surprised when Joe quit that night. You have to get the way a guide's mind works. He's there to get fish. It's his job and he's proud of it. The first man to bring in a tarpon has it all over the rest. Then too the first tarpon is news. It gets in the papers, and naturally all the resorts try to get it.

So Joe quit. He waited until all the other boats had gone out to fish the night tide, and he quit right outside my window after I had put out the light and was going up to bed. I suppose he thought I had gone. The first thing I heard was his voice.

"Sorry to bother you, Mack," he said. "I thought I'd better tell you. I'm through."

"What the hell are you talking about?" That was Mack, and madder than a wet hen. But Joe was beyond caring.

"I'm a fisherman," said Joe stolidly. "I'm no shell-gatherer, and I can think of better things to do just now than picnicking among the fiddler crabs on a beach. Besides Mr. Renwick's here, and he needs a guide. So I'm quitting."

Well, of course, that just isn't done. A guide takes you for better or worse. But Joe had made up his mind.

"I know when I'm licked," he went on stubbornly. "You haven't been in the Pass since you came, and I've yet to hear of a fish being caught on the gulf course. Or in the hotel either. Mind you," he went on, "it's your business. If the young lady doesn't like to fish that's all right with me. Only it happens fishing's my business, and I don't aim to spend the rest of the time just wearing out the seat of my pants."

"Damn it, you're being paid for it," said Mack, savagely.

"Not for wearing out my pants, Mack. I'll bring your tackle up, and you can leave a check at the desk. I'm through."

There is no arguing with Joe when he is in that mood, and Mack knew it. I heard Joe go up the stairs to the lobby, evidently to tell Mr. Renwick, but Mack didn't move. He stood still for a minute. Then he lit a cigarette and started down the beach. I guessed the Jeffries girl wouldn't see him again that night, and I was right. I met her on the way up, looking pretty as a picture and rather breathless, and she asked where he was.

"He was going to play backgammon," she said. "I wonder where he is?"

"The last time I saw him," I said, "he was starting for a walk up the beach."

"A walk? But he said—"

"I don't think he feels like playing games," I said coldly. "You see, he's lost his guide, and I guess it's upset him."

She looked bewildered.

"Why should that upset him?" she inquired. "He hasn't fished anyhow."

"That seems to be the trouble," I told her, and left her standing there.

46

Well, as I say, she didn't see him again that night. I undressed for bed, and as I was raising the window I saw her limping back to the hotel alone. She stopped once to empty sand out of her slippers, and I had a good look at her face. I thought she had been crying.

Then of course the first fish was caught. At one o'clock in the morning I heard a boat horn tooting, and Joe brought old Mr. Renwick in, with the first fish of the year. It weighed only sixty pounds, but it was a tarpon and it was news. Joe didn't look any too happy; but Amy, the telephone operator, phoned the news to the New York papers the next morning, and wires for reservations began to come in from all over the country.

I didn't sleep much that night. Mack had only three days of his leave left, and that brat of a girl had spoiled them for him.

He didn't play golf the next morning. I was in the staff dining room when he came down to breakfast, and as the door into the main dining room was open I could see and hear him as he stopped at her table. She gave him a bright smile.

"It's a perfect day," she said. "If we can get off before the rest —"

"Sorry, my dear," he said. "You'd better get somebody who knows how to play golf and likes it. I don't."

She looked stunned.

"Of course," she said, "if that's the way you feel —"

"That's the way I feel," he told her, pleasantly. "You see, I'll never make a golfer, and I know it.

So I'm going fishing, for a change."

"But I thought—hasn't Joe resigned or something?"

He smiled at that, but it was slightly twisted.

"I wouldn't say he's particularly resigned. He's quit. That's all."

"Then how can you fish, Mack?"

"I'll tell you, if you're interested," he said. "I'm going to dig out some fiddler crabs from the beach, and I'm going to try for sheepshead off the old dock by the golf course. The kids have been getting some there."

She didn't get it. Not even that about the children. And of course she didn't know that to a tarpon fisherman going after sheepshead is as if a tennis champion took up tiddledewinks. She even hoped he would have good luck, although I could see she was puzzled and hurt. Then Minnie came to my table to arrange for a permanent that night, and I missed the rest of it.

Well, as I said at the beginning, I gave Minnie her permanent that night. Dinner had been late, for when the fish are in, meals are served if and when people come for them. Minnie was full of talk. She told me about Mack eating alone that night, and so on.

"He must be feeling terrible," she said. "No boat and no guide."

But I didn't want to talk about him. I was seeing the Pass at night, as I'd seen it now and then when some guide had an evening off: the boats with their white lights like drifting stars, the splash of the fish when they rolled, the blood-chilling snort

48

of a porpoise when he came up to blow close at hand, and the dim outline of the palms. And Mack out of it, sulking alone some place. Not even with the Jeffries girl. I felt uneasy somehow. But there is no shutting Minnie up.

"Slim says he put forty dollars in the fifty-cent machine after dinner and lost it all," she said. "Ouch, you hurt, Ethel."

"That's right."

"What's right?"

"I hurt," I said.

She looked at me, and I pulled myself together. "Somebody's going to get that jackpot soon," I said. "Maybe I'll get my fare North after all."

I got her wrapped and under the machine. Then I borrowed fifty cents from her and went upstairs. But there was no sign of Mack, and after I'd lost the money I went back to Minnie. It was almost one o'clock by that time, and I was dead on my feet. Minnie was peevish.

"What's the idea of leaving me alone?" she said. "What if the place caught fire?"

I didn't answer, for I had just seen a funny thing. I'd seen Mack sneaking down the back stairs, and unless I was seeing things he had his heavy tarpon rod with him. It just didn't make sense. What is more, I realized all at once that a storm was coming up. It's like that down there. One minute it's clear and calm, with the stars as big as saucers. Then the palms begin to rattle, there is a warning shower or two of rain, all at once it's blowing hard, and there is enough thunder and lightning to make one want to crawl under a bed.

I got Minnie shampooed and under the drier. Then I stepped outside. It didn't look too good. The palms had stopped rattling and begun to swish, and there wasn't a star in sight. Far away too I could hear the boats coming back. The Pass is no place to be in a storm.

When I went back the Jeffries girl was in the hall. She hadn't much on under her bathrobe, and she looked young and sort of helpless, if you know what I mean.

"I wonder if you've seen Mr. McKnight?" she said breathlessly. "I've tried to get him on his room telephone. I wanted to tell him something, but he doesn't answer."

I felt sorry for her. She looked like a kid, and she looked worried. Minnie was watching us both, but of course she couldn't hear anything with the drier roaring in her ears.

"The last time I saw him," I said, "he was going up the beach with a tarpon rod in his hand. Don't ask me why. I couldn't tell you."

She seemed relieved.

"Are there tarpon around the island?" she asked.

"Not unless they've got legs to walk here."

All at once she began to cry. She didn't have a handkerchief, so I got her a towel.

"I've been such a fool, Ethel," she said, wiping her eyes. "Why didn't he tell me? I'd have understood. I thought—I thought he just liked playing around."

"Playing your game," I said coldly.

She looked at me.

"I'd have thought more of him if he had played his own," she said.

I remember that now. It didn't register then, because at that moment I heard a boat engine starting up. That was queer, because there wasn't a boat left on the island. Then I remembered the old speedboat tied up at the dock off the golf course, and I knew.

That fishing fool had got the engine going and was on his way to the Pass, storm and all, to fish the two o'clock tide alone.

You've got to know what that means. It takes two people to manage a tarpon. One is the person who has it on the line. He has a man-size job from the start. He's got a fighting devil to try to hold, unless he wants to throw away a hundred and fifty dollars' worth of tackle. And you can't tell what the fish will do. It may come up under and knock a plank of two out of the boat. I've heard of that happening. It may even jump into the boat, in which case it's ten to one somebody is knocked overboard, or gets a broken leg. So the minute a fish is on, the guide starts the engine and keeps moving. Not fast. Just enough to keep the big boy out of mischief.

So now Mack was on his way alone to the Pass in that leaking wreck of a boat. Not only that. The other boats were coming back, which meant that he would be alone in the Pass in a gale of wind; and the Pass in a stiff blow looks like the North Atlantic in a hurricane.

And I knew him. He would get a fish, storm

51

and all.

I guess I was pretty excited.

"Do you hear that boat?" I said. "That's your young man going out to commit suicide. That's what it amounts to. Just hope I can get a boat and a guide there in time. That boat's fast, when it goes at all."

She didn't cry any more. I'll say that for her. She just stiffened.

"I'm going with you," she said.

"You're staying right here," I told her. "I won't answer for what Joe will do if he sees you."

I clean forgot about Minnie. I grabbed a raincoat and headed for the dock. Joe had just come in. He was helping Mr. Renwick out from under the canvas, but when he saw my face he let him go.

"Anything wrong, Ethel?"

"You and your sickly pride!" I yelled, over the wind. "Mack's on his way to the Pass in the old speedboat."

"The goddam jackass," said Joe.

I jumped in and he cast off. But just then the Jeffries girl landed beside me. However, Joe didn't throw her out. There wasn't time. He merely gave her a look of hatred and pushed off.

Well, of course we couldn't catch Mack. He had too good a start for that. But we went all-out to the Pass, and Joe saw him in a flash of lightning before I did. There was a big sea on, waves coming in from the open Gulf so that I could hardly stay in the boat. As for the thing Mack was in, it was riding as if it was half full of water. Joe headed straight for it, and I didn't like his face. He looked scared. He was muttering to himself too, and if I hadn't known him I would have said he was praying.

Then suddenly something leaped out of the water not far from us, and we heard Mack's voice above the wind.

"Keep back, you fool," he shouted. "I'm all right. It's a big one."

He was standing up, trying to hold that excuse for a boat into the sea with one hand and gripping his rod with the other. And he was laughing. I'll never forget that. He hadn't really laughed since he hit the island. Joe had edged up as close as he dared, but when I urged him to go nearer he shook his head.

"If I make him lose that fish he'll kill me," he said.

"He's crazy. You're all crazy!" I yelled. Joe shook his head.

"He'll play it until it's tired," he said. "Then I'll pick him up."

I knew it wasn't any use. They were both fishing fools, and it's against the rules to touch another man's tackle when he has a fish on. All this time the Jeffries girl hadn't spoken a word. I thought she was scared dumb. But I just didn't know her.

Because the next flash of lightning showed no boat and no Mack, and while I was screaming my head off she was taking off her shoes. Joe caught her just in time.

"Stay where you are," he said. "I suppose you can't run a boat?"

53

She didn't answer. She merely went forward in her stocking feet and took the wheel.

"Don't go over until you see him," she said, as quietly as if we weren't alone in the Pass in the middle of the night and a storm on. "Get your searchlight. I'll manage the boat all right."

Well, even Joe says she handled the boat as if she had been born in one. But at first it looked pretty hopeless. It's all right in the Pass when it's smooth and the head of a big loggerhead turtle looks like that of a man swimming; but in that rough water there wasn't a sign of Mack where the boat went down, and even Joe looked hopeless. It was the girl who found him.

She was dead white, but still quiet. Using her head too, for she said:

"What way would that fish go? Toward the Gulf?"

"What the hell does that matter?"

"He might still be holding on to it."

Well, I know it sounds crazy, but that is the way we found him. She took a big circle toward the Gulf, and we picked him up just inside the bar. He was pretty well winded. Joe got him aboard, and if you'll believe it, he still had his rod in his hand. What's more, the fish was still on!

I just went up to the girl and kissed her. Then I shoved her away from the wheel and took it myself. When Mack looked around he saw me there and grinned.

"Good work, Ethel," he said. "Never knew you could handle a boat."

"I can do a lot of things," I told him.

54

He didn't even hear me. He was sneezing and dripping salt water all over the place, but he had only one thing in mind. He sat down in the swivel chair, put the butt of his rod into the rest, took a breath or two and began to pump the fish in. He looked happier than I had seen him since he came.

"Golly," he said. "I feel like myself again, Joe. How much would you say that cockle-shell will set me back?"

I had a chance to speak to the girl. Mack hadn't seen her at all.

"Listen," I said. "I'm sorry about taking that wheel. But you've done enough to him, you and your golf. Better not let him know you saved his life."

She got it that time all right. When at last the fish came in and Joe leaned over the side of the boat with the release hook, Mack saw her for the first time. He looked stunned.

"What on earth are you doing here?" he asked.

And I'll give that girl credit. If she was acting, it was swell. I didn't think she was, however. She was the complete female then, all scared and shaky.

"I was frightened, Mack," she said, in a small voice. "I made them bring me."

"It's no night for you to be out," he told her, all male and disapproving. "What have you got on, anyhow? Get a coat or something. You'll take cold."

I knew then it was all right. He had stopped being a doormat, and from the way she smiled I knew she liked it.

Joe was holding the fish.

"Big boy, Mack," he said. "Looks like a diamond-button to me."

Mack looked down. In the light from the mast the fish was lying on its side. It must have been seven feet long — at least it looked it. Mack stared at it and grinned.

"He gave me a good fight," he said. "Let him go, Joe. I owe him something."

I think Joe's heart almost broke at that. He didn't even measure the fish. He took out the release hook and stood back, and maybe the water on his face was sea-water and maybe not. We all watched as the fish began to move a little, his tail first, then the big smooth muscles of his sides. Even then he stayed awhile, getting his breath, and the girl reached down and touched his silver body with her hand just before he moved off.

"Good-bye," she said.

It gets you, you know. I was darned near crying myself, what with excitement and everything. A game fish and a game man — but what am I rambling about anyhow? If you've never seen it you wouldn't know.

All this time, remember, we'd been rolling about like nobody's business. I felt queasy myself, and I'm a good sailor. It was after we'd started for home that the Jeffries girl spoke.

"Does the Pass ever get much rougher than that?" she asked.

"Not unless there's a hurricane," said Joe.

She laughed. It was a shaky laugh, but it was real enough.

"Then I guess I can fish after all," she said. "I

haven't been seasick at all."

I think that was the first time Mack had looked at her with any real expression since Joe had quit.

"What's this about getting seasick?" he said.

"I used to. Dreadfully. I have to stick to rivers and things. That's the reason I couldn't fish. Not with you anyhow, Mack. I was ashamed to let you know."

If ever I've seen a man with a load off his mind it was Mack just then. He clean forgot that Joe and I were there. He leaned over and put his hand under her chin, so she had to look him.

"Listen, my darling," he said. "Did you really think that a man would care less for you because you up-chucked your last meal? What do you think love is?"

"I don't really know, Mack," she said softly.

I guess he told her. I know I turned my back after that, but from the way he helped her out of the boat when we got back I gathered it was all right. But he stopped me and held out his hand.

"Thanks a lot, Ethel," he said. "If you hadn't been in the boat I guess I would be fighting the sharks about now. Joe too."

"Don't be a fool," I said sharply. "I don't know a thing about—"

And then the girl pinched me. It was a hard pinch. I think I have said she had good strong hands.

"Wasn't she wonderful?" she said. "She heard you start out, too, Mack. If it hadn't been for her—"

Yes, she had learned her lesson all right. Unless

Win McKnight reads this he will always think I saved his life. Maybe I did, at that.

Minnie was still under the drier when I got back. She was sound asleep, but she roused when I went in.

"Where have you been?" she said fretfully. "I've read this whole magazine."

I turned the clock so she couldn't see it.

"Well, you're good and dry," I told her, and took the pins out. That was one set that lasted, if I do say it. She still talks about it. But I got her off at last. She paid me in half dollars and quarters out of her tips, and I locked it away in the cash drawer and started up to bed.

The hotel was quiet. The night clerk was asleep behind the desk and the bar was dark and deserted. The storm was over, too. All I could hear was the dripping of the trees. But there was a light on over the slot machines, and tired as I was I went down again and got a half dollar of Minnie's money. I had a feeling that it might be my lucky night.

It was. I pulled the lever, and in a minute there was silver money all over the place. I'd broken the jackpot.

The Clue in the Closet

The Clue in the Closet

I was ready to make the rounds with Johnny O'Neil that night. Every now and then Johnny calls me up and asks me if I want to see the other side of life, and I always do. It isn't only because in wartime there isn't much else to do. I like Johnny. And after all day at the Red Cross it is a change.

Sometimes I merely sit in his office at headquarters and wait for something to happen. If nothing interesting turns up the detectives sit around and smoke and talk about old cases. It is a shabby room, with holes in the plaster which they gravely tell me are from the bullets they use to scare people into confessions.

"You'd be surprised," they say. "The noise, and thinking maybe the next time they'll be hit. Remember that Chink, Joe?"

I look shocked, because they expect me to. Something mildly interesting comes in now and then, women complaining about their husbands, or a lost child, or a sneak thief, or even a gunman, picked up on suspicion. But most of the time the only excitement is on Saturday nights. That they say is murder night; family fights over the pay envelope, too much to drink because the next day is Sunday, and so on.

Only this was not Saturday. It was a dull Tuesday. I had been going to a dinner which had been called off, and father and I were playing double solitaire when Johnny called up at ten o'clock.

He sounded excited. He is a big good-looking Irishman who had worked his way through college, and my interest in crime amused him. He lived with his mother in a neat small house in Brooklyn, and this was his night to go home to her. I hadn't expected to hear from him.

"Doing anything?" he said over the phone.

"Merely trying to keep father from going out on the town."

Father looked outraged, and Johnny said he would come around and pick me up. When he came in he looked rather grim, and my parent eyed him with suspicion.

"What is it tonight, Lieutenant?"

"Just a round to show Miss Anne the taxi dance high spots. Nothing to worry about, sir."

Father grunted.

"After considerable thought," he said, "I have decided that there was a mistake at the hospital when my child was born. Nothing else will explain her avid interest in the underworld."

Johnny smiled.

"It's better than sitting around in nightclubs."

"It isn't essential that she do either."

"Look," said Johnny. "Maybe a girl gets bored. I wouldn't know. Maybe she wants to write a book. I don't know that either. But I've got an idea that the less you keep her wrapped up in feathers the better she'll be able to take care of herself."

They were still at it when I came down after changing into a plain hat and an old dark suit. Johnny gave me an appraising look.

"You know," he said to father, "she might even be useful some day. She's smart, and she knows the way people like you live. Take a house like this. What do I know about it? But every now and then somebody who lives this way gets killed. Read the papers if you don't believe me."

"I don't read about crime in my newspapers," said father stiffly.

Johnny got me out to the street in a hurry. Usually he moves slowly, like most big men, but I was down the steps and on the pavement before I knew it. I saw at once that something had happened. He didn't have his own car, for one thing. A police car was waiting, with a uniformed driver, and the three of us squeezed into the seat.

"Step on it," said Johnny briefly.

It was a pretty wild ride, but a short one. The car drove up in front of a high stone house, much like our own. There as an officer on duty at the door, and he let us in. I did not know the house, but it was a familiar type: a marble-floored hall, a reception room to the right, a broad iron-railed staircase to the left. Johnny took me into the reception room and closed the door.

"It's not taxi dances tonight, Anne," he said. "I'm going to use you as I said. If you're willing."

"Of course I'm willing. What's it all about, Johnny?"

"Ever hear of Caroline Jennings?"

"Who hasn't?"

"Know her?"

"I've seen her around. It would be hard to miss her."

"Acquainted with her family?"

"No. You know that sort of crowd. They never seem to have any families, or any homes."

"You're in her home now."

"What am I doing here?"

"I'll tell you in a minute. Just now I want you to wash your face. Leave it as shiny as you can. No make-up. What about your hair?"

"I like it this way."

"Sure. So do I," said Johnny imperturbably. "Only it won't do. Stick it up under your hat. And hurry up. We haven't got all night."

This was a new Johnny, his mouth set and his eyes cold. To my own surprise I let him shove me into the powder room next door and close me in there; and when I came out—sans powder, lipstick, rouge and even hair—he didn't even smile. He merely inspected me.

"You'll do," he said. "From now on you're a stenographer, taking some notes for me. And keep your eyes peeled. There's something about this case I don't like."

"What case?" I inquired.

He seemed startled.

"I thought I told you," he said. "The Jennings girl committed suicide here tonight. It looks like suicide. The family says it's suicide. The doctor says it's suicide. Only I don't believe it's suicide."

I was stunned. Even if I hadn't known her I knew a lot about her. She wasn't a bad sort, but she was a publicity hound, if ever there was one. Wherever the crowd was thickest and the noise greatest there was Caroline Jennings. She was no beauty. Take away her extravagant clothes and her make-up and she would look like any pint-size girl anywhere. But the gossip columns always played her up, and she loved it. I would have said she was the last person in the world to kill herself.

Johnny answered my look.

"Shot herself," he said. "Gun beside her, finger-prints on it, door locked and everything. Only it smells to me. Why would she do it? She had everything. And here's the point. I've seen a lot of suicides, but I'm damned if I ever saw a woman kill herself na—without her clothes on. Sometimes it's only a nightdress, but it's something. Mostly they're even fixed up a bit. You know—so they'll look nice when they're found."

The idea of nudity seemed to embarrass him. He looked uncomfortable. "Not even stuff on her face," he said. "Cold cream, believe it or not."

"Maybe she only wanted to be different," I said. "She spent her life doing that."

"Well, look," he said, still more unhappy. "It isn't as though she had a—as though she was much to see, at that. Thin, she was. No curves.

65

No—well, looked like a picked chicken, as a matter of fact."

I sat down. I didn't feel very good.

"But I'm not a stenographer," I said feebly. "What on earth am I to do?"

He looked disappointed.

"Damned if I know what they teach girls these days," he said. "I suppose, if you were put to it, you could make a few squizzles, couldn't you? So they'd look like the real stuff? Then, if you hear or see anything that's not according to Hoyle you can let me know."

"I won't be any use, Johnny," I protested.

He waved a hand.

"Leave that to me," he said. "I've got their statements already. Just keep your eyes peeled."

When we went out into the hall there was a young man in an army uniform sitting there on a hard marble bench. He must have been there when we went in, for he looked at me and blinked his eyes. I didn't blame him. I wasn't the same girl.

"Excuse me, Lieutenant," he said, getting up, "but I've got only a short leave. If you don't need me—"

"Sorry," Johnny said gruffly. "I'll let you off as soon as I can."

He sat down again, looking miserable. And we went up the stairs to the second floor. The layout was rather like ours at home, a big drawing room in front, a library behind it and the dining room, pantry and dumbwaiter at the rear. Johnny put me at the desk in the library and gave me a notebook and pencil.

"Now remember," he said. "This is just a job to you. We're short-handed, and my regular man is off duty. You don't care what's happened here. All you want is to get home and get to bed."

"How true!" I murmured. "How very, very true."

He was not listening. Two men in white coats were carrying down a basket stretcher, with a short tubby man keeping an eye on them. It made me shiver, but Johnny only glanced out.

"Can you come in, doctor?" he said. "I'd like a few words with you."

The doctor came in, looking annoyed.

"I've already told you all I know, Lieutenant," he said. "What's this about?"

He looked at me, and Johnny explained me airily.

"Miss Reilly is helping out," he said. "My man sprained a knee. I just want to verify what I got before. If I remember, you were called at eight o'clock?"

"A little after. Ten minutes or so. I got here before eight-thirty."

"The door was already broken open?"

"Yes. Mr. Jennings and Carlos the butler had tried it. Then they got the young officer from downstairs. He managed it."

"When you got here she was still on the floor? Nobody had touched her?"

"So they said. I examined her and put a sheet over her. That's all. She'd been dead about an hour."

"The gun was still beside the body?"

67

"Yes. I think Wilkinson—that's the army fellow—told them not to touch it. He didn't think she'd killed herself."

"Oh, he didn't think that, eh? Did he say why?"

"Some poppycock about her not being the sort to do it. That's all. How are you going to tell who is going to do a thing like that? Anyhow her door was locked," he finished, less dramatically.

He picked up his bag, but Johnny had not finished.

"Tell me something, doctor. You know her pretty well. You've attended her, I suppose. Was she in the habit of going about"—he glanced at me—"without her clothes?"

"Good God!" The doctor glared. "How do I know? How do I know what young women do today? I understand they go out wearing a dress and nothing under it. It's indecent. As for Caroline, the times I've seen her she's worn adequate clothing, so far as I could tell."

"In bed?"

"She wore a nightdress, or pajamas. I never noticed. She was covered all right."

"Yet she strips to kill herself. Isn't that rather unusual?"

"She was crazy; out of her mind. Too many late hours, too many drinking parties— How they stand it I don't know."

"Only now and then one doesn't?"

"That's right. One doesn't."

I made a few squizzles, but it all seemed, as Johnny would say, according to Hoyle. The doctor said he had given Mrs. Jennings a sedative and

68

hoped she wouldn't be disturbed, and Johnny let him go and took some notes from his pocket.

"Here's who were in the house tonight when the body was found," he said. "Her mother and father, a kid sister, Camilla, and a school friend of hers named Gussie Garrison. The Wilkinson fellow, who claims he wasn't above the lower floor until they sent for him to break open the door. And the servants: four of them, cook, two maids and the old boy who is the butler. None of them knows anything."

"Maybe she did do it herself. After all the way it looks—"

"The way it looks smells," he said shortly. "She's giving a dinner party at a restaurant, followed by the theater. At a few minutes after seven Wilkinson calls to get her. The butler goes up to the fourth floor to notify her. He raps on the door and she says all right. She'll not be long. Twenty minutes later she shoots herself. Does that make sense?"

"How do you know it was twenty minutes later?"

"The two girls were on that floor. They'd been playing basketball at school, and they were taking showers about the time it happened. The sister was in the shower, and the other one, Gussie, was somewhere around. She's panicked, but she says she heard the shot. Didn't know it was a shot, of course. Thought it was the usual backfire. She thinks it was before seven-thirty."

I thought it over. Between seven and seven-thirty at home father and I were either dressing for dinner or to go out. The servants had finished their six o'clock supper downstairs and those who had nothing to do were still at the table. I didn't know the young officer at all, but if he knew where Caroline's room was he could have got upstairs easily enough. Only what about the locked door?

I felt confused and useless, and Johnny came over and patted me on the shoulder.

"It's a tough nut all right," he said. "Don't worry. You may get something yet."

But I didn't get anything at all from Mr. Jennings, who came next. He looked as though he could scarcely stand. He had taken off his dinner coat and put on a dressing gown, but otherwise he was still dressed. He was not only upset, however. He was highly indignant.

"How long is this going on?" he demanded. "Has a family no privacy at a time like this?"

"I'm sorry," Johnny said, and looked it. "I just wondered— Mr. Jennings, would you have said your daughter was the sort to take her own life? I mean, forget the facts as you know them and think of that."

Mr. Jennings sat down, as though he couldn't stand any longer.

"What else am I to think?" he said heavily. "She seemed happy. I didn't approve of the life she lived, but she was of age and she had her own money. She was living on her nerves, of course."

"There was no unhappy love affair? Nothing of that sort?"

"I don't think so."

"And today? Anything happen today?"

"Nothing that I know of. I hadn't seen her. She

always slept late. When I came home tonight she had gone to her room." He stood up. "Why can't you let it rest, Lieutenant?" he said. "Nothing will help her now, or bring her back. I suppose we should have tried to control her, but at least she had the sort of life she wanted—while she had it."

Johnny let him go. He closed the door behind him and came over to me.

"Perfect picture of bereaved father, eh?" he said.

"Perfect."

He grunted.

"They're all like that," he said. "Family and servants. Even Wilkinson. All according to Hoyle. Think Wilkinson knew you? He gave you a queer look down in the hall."

"Who wouldn't?" I said with some bitterness. "Certainly I didn't look like the girl you brought in."

He grinned.

"Well, you do look pretty plain," he said. "Imagine having to look at you like that every morning at breakfast!"

"I don't see why that need worry you."

If he heard me he ignored it. He went out and down the stairs, and I sat alone, drawing a sketch or two in the notebook, as I do when I am puzzled. I was putting a jaw on Johnny's profile when I heard a faint sound outside. I got up quietly and went to the door. A girl was running up the stairs to the next floor. I had only a glimpse of her, but she had Caroline's blonde hair, and I knew it was Camilla. I hadn't a doubt she had been listening from the drawing room, and I was still wondering about it when Johnny and Lieutenant Wilkinson came in.

He was a good-looking man in his late twenties, but he was definitely irritated.

"I don't get this," he said. "Why more questions? I've told you all I know."

Johnny eyed him stonily.

"Why didn't you think she did it herself?"

He looked uneasy.

"I don't know. It looked queer, that's all. I'd had word she was coming down. Then — well, she didn't."

Johnny lit a cigarette and offered him one. I watched them enviously.

"What about her, Wilkinson," Johnny said. "Normal girl? Not an exhibitionist type, or that sort of thing? Don't bother about Miss Reilly. She's used to police stuff."

Lieutenant Wilkinson glanced at me and looked away hastily, as though he couldn't bear the sight. I made a few squizzles.

"She was normal enough," he said. "Just a wild kid with too much money. She knew she wasn't pretty, so she went all out on clothes and parties."

"No love affairs?"

"Not what you mean. Men liked her. She was good fun. But she wasn't in love with anybody, so far as I know. There was one fellow who was crazy about her, but she wasn't interested. Nice fellow, too. Name was Moore. Jason Moore. He killed himself soon after. Turned his plane out to sea and didn't come back."

Johnny was interested.

"Think that would make her commit suicide? Remorse, I mean. Take it pretty hard?"

But Wilkinson shook his head.

"I wouldn't think so. She didn't give a whoop in hell for him."

He told his story—or re-told it—calmly enough. He had arrived at a few minutes after seven. The butler went up and came back with word Caroline would soon be down. But she did not come, and finally, at something after half past seven, he rang the doorbell again and when the butler appeared he sent him up again.

He did not come back at all. After a short time he—Wilkinson—heard banging on one of the upper floors, but he had no idea what it was about. He went out into the hall to listen, and he was still there when the butler came back, looking frightened.

"Mr. Jennings would like you to come upstairs," he said. "Miss Caroline's door is locked and she doesn't answer. She may have fainted."

He had found Mr. Jennings in the upper hall. Mrs. Jennings and the younger sister, Camilla, were there too. Mrs. Jennings was crying. Together—the old man was no use—they broke in the door, and she was lying on the floor. The father had put an arm out to hold his wife back, and Wilkinson was the one who went in. She was dead, of course. He wasn't quite sure what happened next. He saw the small pearl-handled revolver on the floor. He recognized it, but he didn't touch it. He didn't touch anything. Mr. Jennings took his wife downstairs. Camilla had run screaming to her

73

room. The butler was useless. He had collapsed in a chair, and Wilkinson finally got him down to the first floor and told the other servants to get him some whisky.

It was only after all that that he realized they ought to call a doctor.

"Not that it was any use," he said. "But I had an idea it was customary." He gave a wry grin. "I didn't think of the police. Not at first, anyhow."

As for why he had kept guard on the stairs, he got to thinking, as Johnny would have said, that the situation smelled.

"Anyhow, I didn't want the servants prying around," he said. "Not the way she was. I wanted to cover her, but I thought I'd better leave things as they were."

He got up and put out his cigarette.

"If that's all—"

But Johnny had not finished.

"You said you recognized the gun. How was that?"

"She carried it with her at night in her evening bag. Used to show it around. Part of the general idea of being different, I suppose. I remember her pointing it in a nightclub once. There was a riot."

Johnny passed that over. He asked if the key was in the door, and Wilkinson said it was.

"We all heard it fall when we first tried to break the lock," he said positively.

He stood while Johnny fired further questions at him. He had not known Caroline well, but he had seen her around a lot. Outside of leaving the reception room to ring the doorbell a second time, and when he heard the noise overhead, he had stayed there with the door closed the rest of the time. No, he didn't know the house at all. He had never been there before. He had thought of telephoning the restaurant that they would be late, but he didn't know where to find a telephone.

Johnny shifted ground.

"This Jason Moore a friend of yours?"

"I know him pretty well. Yes."

"Upset you when he killed himself?"

"It didn't seem necessary. He was an only son. It pretty nearly drove his mother crazy."

I rather liked him. He looked like a good soldier and a nice boy. But Johnny wasn't being fooled by any uniform, especially since he had broken his heart to get into the service himself.

"Now look, Wilkinson," he said, "here's the picture. The front door was locked. The servants were in the back of the house. They alibi each other. The family was dressing. Only one person in this house is unaccounted for. That's yourself."

Wilkinson stiffened.

"So I killed her!" he said. "Why? Because of Jason Moore? Don't be a damned fool, Lieutenant. I hadn't a reason in the world. As for my being the only person loose in the house tonight, maybe that's true, maybe it isn't. Somebody used the elevator while I was waiting for her. I heard it."

He stuck to that. He had heard a noise after he had waited a quarter of an hour or so. At first it puzzled him. Then he realized that it was the humming of an elevator. He had thought it was Caroline coming down, but after a minute or so he knew the car was going up instead. He hadn't given it any thought, except to hope it meant she was dressed at last.

"Only it didn't come down again," he said. "It was on the fourth floor when we broke in the door. It was there until the doctor arrived. It went down for him."

Johnny sent him downstairs to wait again and turned to me. He looked disheartened.

"Maybe I'm crazy," he said. "Maybe she did kill herself. Maybe she didn't think it mattered whether or not she had any clothes on. Or maybe she thought her last bit of publicity might as well be a good one. What about that elevator? The servants use it?"

"Not in our house. They're supposed to have legs."

"Good girl," he said approvingly. "That's what I need. So the servants didn't use it. Then who did? Mr. and Mrs. Jennings were in their rooms on the third floor, the girls were on the fourth. Maybe Wilkinson himself used it."

"And then got out through a locked door!"

"Oh, damn the door," he said resignedly. "Well, we still have the kid sister and Gussie. After that, you can let down your hair and go home." He grinned. "What are you going to tell father when you get there?"

"So far as he's concerned, I'm in a ten-cent dance hall, asking the girls if their feet hurt. I think the sister was in the next room a while ago, Johnny. Probably listening."

"Probably," said Johnny indulgently. "Skinny

blonde girl?"

"That's the one."

He rang for Carlos, and the butler came to the door. He was an old man, practically doddering and obviously shaken. He said he had not used the elevator that night, or ever. Also that the front door was always locked. No, he had not admitted anyone but Lieutenant Wilkinson. I made a few squizzles, but he paid no attention to me whatever. He went up the stairs to send the girls down, and Johnny lit a cigarette and lapsed into silence.

It was some time before the girls appeared. They had been in bed, and they came in together, in their nightgowns under dressing gowns, and with their feet in bedroom slippers. Camilla was the girl I had seen on the stairs, and I gathered that the quiet little redhead behind her was Gussie. They looked about sixteen, and Camilla was shrilly furious.

"What's the idea?" she said. "I don't know a damned thing, and neither does Gussie. If Caroline wanted to shoot herself that was her business, wasn't it?"

But she was not as tough as she pretended. Her eyes were red with crying. She came over to the desk for a cigarette, eying me coldly as she did so, and her hands were shaking.

"As for Gussie, why bring her in? She hardly knew Caroline. What business is it of hers? And why the police anyhow? You'd think we could have some peace here tonight."

"Just a few questions," said Johnny smoothly. "Why don't you sit down? I'm not dangerous."

He gave her his best smile, and Johnny's best smile is something. She looked rather sheepish, but she did sit down. Only Gussie remained standing.

"I think I'll go back to bed," she said. "You don't need me, do you?"

I took my first good look at Gussie then, and surprised myself. For if she was not on the verge of the screaming meemies no girl ever was. She was not shaking. She was rigid. And she had gone to bed with her lipstick on. Even Camilla had cleared her face, but not Gussie.

"It won't take a minute," said Johnny soothingly. "Just where were you and so on. I understand you heard the shot, Miss Gussie?"

"I never said that. I said I heard a noise. I thought it was a backfire."

"That was while Miss Camilla here was in the shower?"

"Yes. I'd had mine."

They were less scared now. Even Gussie had relaxed a little. But something puzzled me. I made a note of it and called to Johnny.

"Just a moment, Lieutenant," I said. "I've written in these times as you suggested. Will you look at them?"

He came over and glanced down, his face impassive. "O.K. as far as I know," he said, and turned back to Gussie.

"I've just remembered," he said. "You were not in the hall when the door was broken down, were you?"

"Why should I be?"

78

"I see. Just where were you?"

"In the library, reading."

She was doing it well, I thought, but she knew something. She was scared stiff again.

"Remember what you were reading?"

"Just something I picked up. I was waiting for Cammy."

"You heard all the noise. Mr. Jennings banging on the door, people running about, and you went on reading?"

"I didn't say that either," she said, goaded. "I just didn't think it was any of my business."

"And it's none of your business either, Mr. Policeman," Camilla broke in. "Just because you wear a uniform isn't any reason for your acting like this. Why shouldn't she stay where she was?"

"Look," said Johnny, losing patience at last, "if you two kids are trying to put something over on me, forget it. I'm not that easy. What are you both scared about? What's the story? Come on, speak up. What do you know?"

They didn't know from nothing, or so they said in just that language. Or Camilla did. Gussie had lapsed into a dazed silence. She looked pretty sick, and I began to be sorry for her. Johnny let them go at last, and Camilla's parting shot was typical.

"You're going to get into trouble if you don't take that policeman away from upstairs," she said from the door. "If you find him knocked out you'll know who did it."

Which was the first intimation I had had that Caroline's room was under guard. Camilla banged out of the room, and Johnny eyed me.

"How did you get on to Gussie?"

"She's scared to death. And why wasn't she around when the door was broken down? Camilla was there, but nobody mentioned Gussie."

"But good Lord, a kid like that!"

"She isn't a baby. She's a good sixteen. Maybe more. And she can read, you know."

He looked puzzled.

"Listen, Johnny," I said patiently, "if Caroline didn't kill herself somebody wiped the gun and put her prints on it. These children as you call them read detective stories. They'd know about that. Probably the doorknobs were wiped too. How about them?"

"Read detective stories yourself, don't you?" He grinned wryly. "No prints at all on the inside knob. Not even Caroline's. That's when I began to get ideas."

But he refused to bring Gussie into the picture. Sure she was scared. So was Camilla. So would any teen-age girl be scared. He wasn't sure I wasn't scared myself. I didn't say anything. I got up, feeling tired and confused.

"Can I see the room, Johnny?"

He shrugged.

"Sure, if you like. Nothing there." He picked up my notebook and looked at it. "Squizzles is right," he observed. "Who's the guy with the jaw?"

"You," I told him. "Imagine having to look at that jaw every day at breakfast."

"It's a libel," he said. "I have a bright and shining morning face. I'll show you some time."

He didn't follow that up, however. He put the

book in his pocket, and we went out to the elevator. It moved slowly, making a definite humming sound. Johnny listened to it.

"How far away do you think you could hear this thing?"

"Two or three floors, I imagine."

He shook his head.

"Funny," he said. "So the servants are supposed to have legs! Then who the hell did Wilkinson hear using it?"

The door opened quietly on the fourth floor. The light was still on in the girls' room at the back of the house, and the officer on a chair outside Caroline's door was half asleep. He was a middle-aged man, and in spite of Camilla's threat he appeared undamaged.

"Everything all right, Jenkins?" Johnny asked.

"All right, Lieutenant. The skinny blonde girl wanted to get into the room. Said her sister had borrowed something of hers she needed. I didn't let her in."

"Right," said Johnny.

He was thoughtful, however. Evidently he did not like the idea of Camilla's trying to get into Caroline's room. "What do you suppose that's about?" he inquired. But he didn't expect an answer, and he got none.

Caroline's room looked much as I had expected, as if she had merely used it when there was no place else to go. But except for the stain on the carpet and the bed torn up when the doctor had taken a sheet from it, it was fairly neat. Certainly it looked as though she had meant to go out that night. A silver evening dress hung over the back of a chair, the slippers to match were near it, and her evening bag was on the dressing table, open.

"That's where she carried the gun, according to Wilkinson," Johnny said.

I nodded. I was looking at the dressing table. It was covered with cream jars and perfume bottles, but it was very orderly. The gold-backed brushes lay in a row, the jars and bottles were grouped. There was only one incongruous thing. A large powder puff, the sort I myself used for bath powder, lay beside the evening bag. Johnny was watching me.

"Well?"

"It's the puff," I said. "It looks as though she put it there herself."

"Why not?"

"It doesn't belong there. A woman powders herself in the bathroom. The stuff flies, you know. She doesn't want it on the carpet."

"So what?"

"I don't know. Maybe she wouldn't care, if she was going to kill herself. Or maybe she was using it in the bathroom when someone knocked at the door. Someone she knew. Someone she didn't mind seeing without her clothes."

He whistled.

"So that's what you think!" he said. "Back to the kid sister, I suppose."

"Or someone who said she was the kid sister. It might have been Gussie."

He shook his head.

"Damned if I believe it," he said. "They put on

all the airs of grownups, but they're children just the same. All the tough talk doesn't make them adults, or killers. Not girls raised like these, anyhow."

"All right," I said shortly. "Find out if anybody saw the Garrison girl in the library when she said she was there. Ask the butler. He passed the door at least three times."

He was still skeptical, but he went out to locate Carlos, and left me alone. I didn't like it much. I felt ineffectual, and the intimate belongings of another girl—so like my own—made me rather sick. But I knew I would have to look around. What had Camilla wanted from the room? If I knew that, and why both girls were half hysterical, I might learn something.

I forced myself to move around. There was nothing much to see, however. Only in the bathroom the water was still in the tub, and the air reeked of bath-salts. Her towel was on the floor, too. Certainly if Caroline had set the stage for a suicide she would have done better than that. There is nothing dramatic about dead bath-water.

I looked around the room. Whatever Camilla had wanted I could not identify it. I looked into the clothes closet, but except that a dress near the front had fallen from its hanger it was orderly. It housed Caroline's huge and dazzling wardrobe: the furs, the dresses, the evening coats, the negligees. Especially the negligees, so easy to slip on, to cover a thin not too attractive body when it was found. Only Caroline had not expected to be found. She had not killed herself. I knew that as soon I saw the dress on the floor and the hanger from which it had fallen.

When Johnny came in I was sitting on a chair because my knees felt weak. He didn't notice.

"He didn't see her," he said. "Says he used the stairs. Didn't look into the library at all. That doesn't mean she wasn't there."

I could see that he was annoyed with me. The girls didn't fit into any pattern of crime that he knew, and he was even more annoyed when I managed to speak.

"I hope you don't mind, Johnny. I'd like to speak to Gussie."

"Gussie! You've got it in for that kid, haven't you?"

"I just want to talk to her."

He was furious. He stalked out, and I could hear shrill protests from the girls' room. When he came back they were both behind him, looking more like children than ever. Camilla put up a bluff, however.

"I'd like to know who you people think you are," she screeched. "Just as we were trying to sleep—"

"With all the lights on?" I asked.

She gave me a hard look.

"Why are you mixing in this?" she demanded. "I thought you were a stenographer. Who are you?"

"Never mind about that. I want to talk to Gussie."

"Gussie's not talking."

I was sorry for her. She reached around and took Gussie's arm, and I felt like the Gestapo. Johnny was looking bewildered.

84

"I'm afraid you'll have to talk, Gussie," I said. "You see, I know you were in that closet."

Gussie went white to the lips.

"I didn't kill her," she said. "I didn't. I wouldn't kill anybody. I've never even shot a gun. I don't know how."

"But you were in the closet when it happened."

She nodded dumbly. I opened my hand and produced a hair-net. Not the usual one, a heavier one, reddish brown in color, to match Gussie's hair. Just such a net I had used at school for basketball, or to set my hair after I had washed it. She gave it an agonized look.

"So what?" said Camilla stormily. "She got out that dress for Caroline. Caroline asked her to, and her net caught on a hanger. You can't pin a murder on her for that."

Johnny was staring at me as if he had never seen me before. Not too agreeably, either. I tried to ignore him.

"I haven't said she murdered anybody," I told Camilla. "Now shut up and keep out of this. It's all right, Gussie. All we want is the truth. You were in the closet when someone shot Caroline. Did you see who it was?"

She shook her head. "The door was closed," she said.

"And you were still in the closet when the door was broken down, weren't you? You got out when Mr. Jennings took Mrs. Jennings away and while Lieutenant Wilkinson helped the butler downstairs."

She nodded again, her poor young face agonized.

"I'd fainted," she said with stiff lips. "I heard the shot, and I fainted. I often faint. I'd gone into the closet to get Caroline something to put around her before she opened the door."

"Who came in, Gussie? Who opened the door?"

"I don't know," she said. "I don't know. I don't know, I tell you."

And at that she proceeded to go into as fine a bit of screaming hysteria as I had heard in a long time. There was no quieting her. Johnny at last picked her up and carried her back to bed, and Camilla, after a murderous look at me, followed. When he came back Johnny looked bewildered.

"Now let's get this, Anne," he said. "Don't tell me you think the girl shot Caroline Jennings. I don't believe it."

"She knows who did it. Maybe she fainted. I think she did. She grabbed at a dress as it fell. It's still on the floor. That's probably when her hairnet caught on the hanger, too. But she didn't faint right away. She did a first-class job of cleaning up for somebody before she did."

"That child! Don't be an idiot, Anne."

"Listen, Johnny," I said patiently. "I didn't want to come here tonight. I wish I was at home in bed this minute with cold cream on my face and a good book to read. But I'm here and I'm going through with it. Who wiped the prints off that gun and put Caroline's on it? Who wiped the doorknobs? If Gussie didn't do it, who did?"

"She fainted."

"All right, have it your own way. I don't think it

was the shot that made her faint. That's all."

"Then what did?"

"Suppose she knows who killed Caroline. Suppose she cleans up as well as she can in a hurry. Then she has to get out. But what happens? With Caroline dead on the floor the butler comes up a second time. He bangs on the door and calls, and Gussie is trapped. She makes for the closet and faints. She's still there when they break the door in. Nobody looks, so she stays there."

"Are you telling me Camilla killed her own sister?"

"No," I said wearily. "Maybe she did. I wouldn't know. All I say is that Gussie knows who did it." I got up. "I'm tired, Johnny," I told him. "I'm tired and sick. I want to go home."

He nodded absently.

"I'll take you," he said. "Then I'll come back. Those girls are going to talk."

I wasn't so sure. Girls are stubborn and loyal, and I had an idea that Gussie wouldn't have talked if she was faced with torture. But in the elevator Johnny seemed to realize that I was still around.

"You look like the wrath of heaven," he said. "I hope to God your father's gone to bed."

There was a mirror in the elevator, and I fixed my face as well as I could. I still looked dreadful, but I didn't care. Johnny didn't care either. He put his arms around me and kissed me.

"Just to make you feel better," he said, and grinned.

I think we had both forgotten Wilkinson until we saw him sitting forlornly in the hall. He got up and tried to smile.

"This is a poor way to spend my bit of leave," he said. "What's the idea of keeping me?"

Johnny stopped in front of him. He was all policeman again.

"I've got a murder on my hands, Lieutenant," he said. "I don't think you're going anywhere tonight. Do you happen to know a girl named Gussie Garrison? I suppose her name's Augusta."

"Never heard of her," he replied promptly.

"Sure of that, are you?"

"I've said so, haven't I?"

He was angry. He stared at Johnny and Johnny stared back. They were about of a height, only Johnny was heavier. The officer at the door took a step toward them, but there as no quarrel. Johnny shrugged.

"Just thought you might know her," he said. "I'll be back soon, then maybe we can let you go."

I think I dozed between the two big men on the way back. But I remember Johnny saying that if the elevator was on the fourth floor when they found Caroline, then whoever killed her must have used the back stairs to get away. He was still exonerating the girls, of course. But I was too exhausted to talk. And father was awake when he took me in. Johnny hadn't wanted to come in. He said he had plenty to do that night without fathers glaring at him and thinking the worst. But he did come in, and father gave me one look and turned on him.

"Is this the way you return my child to me?" he demanded. "Has she been in a riot, or fighting a fire?"

Johnny looked sheepish.

"I'm sorry, sir. She did a bit of police work tonight."

"Police work?" said father, scandalized. "Good God, why do I pay taxes? Why can't the police do their own dirty work?"

But of course this was just father. He was pouring Johnny a drink while he talked and moving a copy of the Social Register out of the way while he did it. I picked up the book. It occurred to me that Gussie might be in it. So far all I knew was her name. And she was in it!

I remember feeling very queer when I had found her, and that father looked up and saw me. The next thing I knew Johnny was carrying me to the sofa, and father was pouring some of his best whisky down my throat. I sat up irritably.

"Stop it," I said. "I didn't faint. I just saw something in the Register."

"I have never regarded it as a dramatic publication," said father, shaken but doing his best. "However, if you say so—"

But Johnny had the book and the place. I knew what he was reading: Garrison, Mr. and Mrs. William D. (Helen Moore) Lieutenant Jason Moore. Miss Augusta Garrison. Johnny looked at me. Father stared at us both.

"So that's it," said Johnny.

"That's it," I said dully.

"Perhaps," said father, "if I understood what all this is about it might be easier. What is *it?*"

Johnny looked at him soberly.

"We've had a murder tonight, sir," he said. "A girl was shot. It looks as though this Mrs. Garrison might have done it. Her daughter was in the house at the time."

Father looked profoundly shocked. People in the Register simply did not do such things.

"You see," said Johnny, "her son by a first marriage committed suicide on account of this girl. It looks as though tonight she was admitted to the house by the daughter, and she killed the girl. The daughter tried to cover up for her, poor kid. And she pretty nearly got away with it, too. If it hadn't been for Anne here—"

The telephone rang. Father picked it up and handed it to Johnny. He listened.

"I see," he said. "Well, I guess that settles something. All right, I'll be around."

He turned and faced us, his face sober.

"Gussie wasn't so successful after all," he said. "Mrs. Garrison has just been identified at the morgue. She fell under a bus tonight."

All I could think of was Gussie doing all those desperate things to save her mother, and then failing after all. When Johnny came over and put his arms around me, I simply put my head on his shoulder and wept. Father poured himself another drink, as though he needed it, and glared at us both.

"Perhaps," he said, "when you two have ceased to ignore my elderly blushes, you will tell me who was killed tonight. Or does it matter?"

I stopped crying and looked at him.

"It was Caroline Jennings, father," I said. "You

know. Caroline Jennings."

"And who," said father incredibly, "is — or was — Caroline Jennings?"

Test Blackout

Test Blackout

Halliday stopped in the hall and laid down, in order, his old steel helmet, his trench coat, his flashlight, and his automatic. Thus denuded, as it were, he became merely a man of forty-five, slightly stooped as to shoulder and with the faintly defeated look so common in business men nowadays.

The living room door was closed. With a glance to see that his equipment was out of sight he opened it and stood in the doorway. The four women around the bridge table looked up.

"I guess I'd better go, Laura," he said apologetically. "The blackout begins pretty soon."

Laura was dealing. He noticed that she was wearing her diamond wrist watch. She did not look up.

"All right," she said. "Go on out and play." She picked up her cards and looked at them. "I'm passing," she said.

The other three women passed. The cards went down. Halliday stood in the doorway, apparently forgotten.

"About those curtains—" he said uncomfortably. "Don't forget them, will you? I mean"—as Laura looked up resignedly—"it's a real blackout. No lights anywhere in this district. When you hear the siren—"

"Good heavens!" said Laura. "As if I've heard about anything else all day!" She smiled at the other women. "He's going out to save the town, girls. What will you bet he's got his tin helmet in the hall?"

Halliday flushed. The girls laughed. They were stout middle-aged women, overdressed and smug. He thought of the other women he knew at the post, who carried on jobs all day and gave their evenings and often their nights to watching over the city. But it was a long time since he had argued with Laura, or with Laura's friends.

"It does seem silly," said one of them. "It's hard to get enough men for a dinner party these days. I'm going to bid something. Let's see."

They had forgotten him entirely. He went out, closing the door behind him, and feeling slightly ridiculous, as though he had been caught playing with tin soldiers. He stood for a minute looking at himself in the hall mirror. He bore very little resemblance to the boy who had gone to France in 1917, singing The Old Gray Mare, with variations, and what he would do to the Kaiser when he got to Berlin. The light shone down on the thin hair on top of his head, and on the slight bulge below his belt. He tried holding in the bulge, but after a minute or so it was painful, and he let it go with a sigh of relief.

The trench coat was tight and smelled to heaven of moth balls, and the helmet had a tendency to slide down over his ears. He had had more hair when he wore it in France. But any hope that the combination would turn him into a dashing military figure died within him. He still looked what he was, a patient, slightly hopeless, middle-aged man, puffy under the eyes from the night life which Laura insisted upon, and too little business, which he blamed on his government and the New Deal.

He looked at his watch. He was still too early. The first signal was to come by telephone at ten, and it was only nine forty-five. Feeling in his pockets he found he had his tin whistle—purpose unknown—his flashlight, the end covered with thin blue paper, and his screwdriver. He looked at the last wryly. Fool thing, that every light in town had to be put out by hand. First you unscrewed the small door in the base of the pole. Then you reached in and turned off the fuse. Some of the wardens had already unscrewed the doors and then conveniently lost the screws. The police had gone around pasting bits of adhesive plaster to hold the doors shut, but even the plaster disappeared. Well—

The door behind him opened. It was Laura. She laughed when she saw him.

"I wish you could see yourself!" she said. "I hope nobody we know gets a look at you. Listen, Jim, I need some money."

He looked at her. It seemed to him lately that Laura had changed, or perhaps he was seeing her for the first time. It had been different when they lived out of town, and he had commuted. She had had a garden then, and at night when he went home they would play two-handed solitaire, or go to the movies, or listen to the radio. But in 1929 he had been too busy to commute. Anyhow he had been making a lot of money. So they had moved in, and now where were they?

Laura's voice was irritable.

"Did you hear me, Jim? I need some money."

"I gave you some this morning."

"It's gone. I can't run a place of this size on nothing."

He unbuttoned the trench coat and pulled out his wallet.

"How much do you need?"

"Twenty. If I lose more I can give a check."

This was his time, to tell her that there was no more money, that he was giving up the car, that they would have to leave the apartment when the lease was up. Even that he might close the office and try to get back into the service again. But he did not do it. He opened the wallet.

"That's all I have."

"You used to carry a lot of money."

"That was when I had it to carry," he said wearily.

But Laura did not hear him. She went back into the living room and closed the door.

The telephone still had not rung. He stood still, looking out the window at the river below, at the stone-paved street, quiet now, which rumbled all day with the noise of trucks moving to and from the line of sheds and wharves. By one of those inexplicable shifts of population the riverfront had suddenly become fashionable. Huge apartments stood cheek by jowl with ancient houses and tenements, rickety and inflammable. One incendiary bomb, and they would burn and burn fast. And beyond them, across the street, were the wharves where ships were loaded with material for Europe, for Russia and the South Pacific. At least he hoped for the South Pacific.

There was a ship there now. It was out in the river, dark save for her riding lights. Waiting for the tide, probably, to slide out and meet her convoy somewhere, and to hope to get across. He wondered what it would be like to be on her, facing catastrophe; men staring across the black waters at night, working, eating and sleeping always under the shadow of death. A white ribbon coming across the water, the ship trying to escape the torpedo, and then—

He began slowly to put on his equipment. The telephone still had not rung. He made a final survey of the apartment: the maids' rooms closed and undeniable snores from inside; the drawn window shades, the sand, the stirrup pump, long-handled shovel and asbestos gloves which Laura considered a part of the general hysteria. Then he took off his helmet, which was hurting his head, and sat down on a stool in the pantry where there was a telephone.

Maybe Laura was right, and he was a fool. He had become a warden largely on impulse. It had been one of their rare nights at home, and Laura had gone disgustedly to her room. Out of sheer loneliness he had taken a late walk along the riverfront, and a youth in a cap with a white brassard on his arm had been standing at the corner. It was bitterly cold, and in spite of his heavy mackinaw he looked half frozen.

Halliday had stopped. There was nothing to warn him that by doing just that he was to change the course of his entire life. He had merely stopped.

"What's the idea?" he said. "Red Cross?"

"Air warden, Mr. Halliday. Just in case of trouble."

Halliday looked surprised.

"Do I know you?" he said. "Or should I?"

The boy—he was little more than that—smiled.

"I'm your milkman. Name's Kelly. I've seen you once in a while, coming home. I get around pretty early, you know."

Halliday felt uncomfortable. He cleared his throat.

"Looks as though you don't get much sleep," he said.

Kelly grinned.

"I'm not on every night. But somebody's got to do it. This river, for instance. They'd like to get a ship or two."

"Then you think they'll come?"

"It's likely, isn't it? Even if they don't there are plenty of them here already."

Laura was massaging cream into her face when he went back to the apartment. She had rolled her hair into aluminum curlers, and was now patiently patting her face. It was to the sharp slap of the patter, familiar as it was, that he told her. She stared at him in the mirror.

"Air warden?" she said suspiciously. "Out all night, I suppose. What am I to do while you're parading the streets and feeling important? Sit here and twiddle my thumbs?"

"I'm over age, Laura," he said. "If I can do my bit —"

"Saving the world for democracy!" she jeered. "The way you did before! All you brought back from that was a game leg and a medal. Lots of good they did you."

He became an air warden the next afternoon. That is, he gave two character references and filled in a questionnaire. On the line which read occupation he thought for a minute. Then he wrote in, "brokerage business, if any."

"Like that, is it?" said the officer, reading it.

"Like that," Halliday said drily.

After that, to his surprise, he was fingerprinted.

"It won't hurt," said the officer. "Just relax, and let me do the work."

So Halliday had relaxed, as much as was possible for a man who had been tight as the skin of a drum for thirteen years, but Laura had taken it rather hard when his card came and he handed it to her. It showed a stamp-size photograph of him, with a slight squint and the light from above focussed on his thinning hair; and it stated that the Police Department of the city now recognized that he was appointed and hereby authorized to perform the duties of Post Warden in Precinct 15,

Zone 2.

"What does it mean?" she said. "Are you telling me you've been fool enough to join that thing after all? At your age?"

"I'm not senile, Laura."

But she was still resentful. He had not been called to duty yet, and that night they had made the usual dreary round. He had spent too much money and had had more than he needed to drink, and at the doorway of the apartment building they met young Kelly with a rack of milk bottles.

Kelly grinned cheerfully.

"Morning, Mr. Halliday," he said. "Hear you've joined us. Glad to know it."

"So that's one of your new friends," Laura said coldly, as they got into the elevator. "You might ask him up for a cocktail some time."

To his surprise he had found himself liking his new job. He had never known anybody in the neighborhood. Now he found himself in a cross section of democracy. The officer on the beat wandered in sometimes to warm his hands. The heavy man with the scar turned out to be Higgins, his grocer. The cheerful individual with red hair was the local undertaker. And the women ranged from middle-aged widows, evidently well off, to stenographers and salesgirls who worked all day and were willing to work at the post all night.

When once a week he took the night watch at his post, from two until six in the morning, a little old gentleman who suffered from insomnia would wander in and let him take a nap.

"Can't sleep anyhow," he would say. "I'll call you

if the phone rings."

He was less lonely than he had been for years. He learned how to put out an incendiary bomb. He learned how to bandage, to care for fractures, even to give artificial respiration. But Laura remained resentful. When one day there arrived with the grocery order a jar of brandied peaches, with a slip fastened to it which read "Compliments of Higgins & Company," she eyed it suspiciously.

"What does it mean?"

"Mr. Higgins is an air warden at my post."

"I see. Well, you'll get it on the bill some way. I know these people."

He wondered if she did. He was liking them a lot, men and women. Especially he liked young Kelly. He and Kelly both patrolled the waterfront. Each had two blocks, and sometimes they took them together. Kelly, it appeared, wanted to enlist in the army, but he had a small boy at home and his wife had died when the youngster was born. A woman took care of him during the day, but he was alone at night.

"A fellow doesn't know what to do," he said. "I'd like to kill me a few Germans or Japs, but what about the boy?"

"What about him now?" said Halliday, rather appalled. "Suppose we do get a bombing, and you're out?"

"He knows what to do," said Kelly. "He's four. He's to get out in the hall and sit on the floor, He'll do it, too. He's a smart kid."

By Christmas Halliday had fallen into the routine, and was feeling better than he had in years.

He was even sleeping, as he had not slept since '29; perhaps not since the last war, when he had found it possible to sleep standing up, or even on the march. And he had lost the sense of loneliness which he had had for so many years. He knew the neighborhood now, and it knew him. Even the police.

"Hiya, Halliday. Any bombs tonight?"

They would grin at him, these big uniformed men, sometimes stop and talk to him.

"How's the brokerage business these days?"

"Shot to hell. How's crime?"

At Christmas Laura bought herself a diamond-studded wrist watch as his gift to her, and the day before he stopped in at a toy shop and sent a small electric train to Kelly's boy.

Kelly was smiling when they met that night on the waterfront.

"Wish you'd seen him," he said. "Talk about excitement! But you shouldn't have done it, Mr. Halliday."

"I liked doing it," Halliday said. "I have no children of my own."

But as the weeks went on and nothing happened, interest in the work began to fall off. They had no money and no equipment, and orders given by the city one day were canceled the next. Halliday grimly held on. So did Kelly. Then had come the idea of a test blackout.

"It might revive some interest in the job," said the senior warden worriedly. "We'll make it noisy. Maybe have an 'incident,' if I can get a smoke bomb or two, and an empty house to use it in. Get out the fire engines too, and an ambulance. I'll have to have permission, of course."

So this was the night.

Halliday roused himself and looked at his watch. He still had five minutes. He snapped the brassard on his left arm and put on his helmet. Below on the river the ship still lay, but now there was smoke rising from her funnels. She was going out, then. Loaded with troops perhaps, crowded into her huge black hulk, sleeping in tiers one above the other. If he had had a son—

He went forward. The game was still going on, and Laura looked up as he opened the door.

"Look," she said. "What did I tell you girls? Helmet and all!"

He smiled his patient rather tired smile.

"Orders," he said. "Don't forget the blackout, Laura. And the curtains. When you hear the siren—"

But Laura was not listening.

"It's a laydown," she said triumphantly, and spread her cards. When she finally looked up the telephone was ringing in the hall, and Halliday had gone.

The elevator boy eyed him with surprise as he went down.

"Sure look like a war tonight, Mr. Halliday," he said, grinning.

"Well, if you're interested, we've got a war," Halliday said shortly.

He felt better when he got to the post. The place was crowded with men and women. There was a sense of expectancy over them all, and the senior

105

warden looked tense, even pale.

"Now listen, everybody," he said. "We are going to reproduce as nearly as possible real raid conditions. Our job as you know is to see that the district is blacked out, to help the police, to avoid panic and get people under cover. We have permission to turn off the street lights in our sector, so have your screwdrivers ready." There was laughter at that. "There will be an 'incident' on Cross Street. Report it here, and for God's sake don't let anybody get hurt. The people have been notified, so there will be no panic. And—I guess that's all."

The telephone rang. The crowd stiffened. The senior warden lifted the receiver.

"Air raid headquarters," he said. "Post 2." He listened, and suddenly became human. "Okay," he said, and hung up.

"All right," he said. "On your way, everybody. I'm staying here."

They pounded on, and as Kelly and Halliday reached the corner they heard the wailing of the fire engine a block or two away, and behind them both house and street lights began to go out. Halliday had some trouble with the first lamps on the waterfront, and Kelly helped him. When they straightened up, Kelly's eyes were on the apartment house overhead.

"Can you beat it?" he said. "Look at those windows!"

Halliday looked up, and a surge of fury shook his whole body. Laura had not closed the curtains after all.

"That's my apartment," he said thickly. "I'll go

back and telephone. Carry on with the lamps, will you?"

It was more than a block back to the post. Up the dark street apparently the "incident" was already occurring. Somebody had set off a Fourth of July bomb, and a red flare was burning. From an empty house black smoke was pouring, and in the glare two men with a stretcher were running along the pavement. But Halliday hardly noticed. He was consumed with anger when he reached the post. He shoved aside the senior warden, who was watching from the doorway, and shot to the telephone. It was some time before Laura answered. He could see her, looking annoyed, laying down her cards, moving languidly across the room.

"Wouldn't you know it?" she would be saying. "Right in the middle of a hand."

He was almost inarticulate when he finally heard her voice, sharp and irritated.

"Hello. Mrs. Halliday speaking."

"What the hell are you doing with the lights on?" he shouted.

"Don't you talk to me like that. I just forgot them."

"Forget them thirty seconds more and the police will be after you," he said grimly, and hung up.

The waterfront was dark when he got back. Kelly had put out the street lamps, and the long line of docks was black. Only the riding lights of the ship hung over the faint slate-gray of the river. He looked up, to see that Laura had finally closed the curtains, and he drew a long breath of relief.

But there was no sign of Kelly. He had gone on,

probably. Well, the thing was done; was going off well, apparently, except for Laura! He started to light a cigarette, remembered, and put his case back in his pocket. He listened for the sound of footsteps; Kelly in the next block. There was no such sound, however, and as his eyes grew accustomed to the darkness, he walked in that direction. It was some time before he realized that Kelly was not there. Was not anywhere, in fact. He had turned off four lamps, Halliday's two and his own, and then he had disappeared.

Halliday crossed the empty street. Perhaps he had seen a light on one of the piers and had gone to notify the watchman. He stood still, listening. The siren had ceased for some time, and the only sound now was the lapping of the water as a sharp wind blew it against the pilings. There was an open shed here, and he felt his way into it cautiously.

"Kelly!" he said. "Where are you?"

There was no answer. His uneasiness increased. Suppose he had gone into the shed, underestimated his distance and fallen into the water? He moved on, feeling his way, unwilling to turn on his flashlight until the staccato sounds of the engine would indicate the end of the blackout. And he was almost at the end of the shed when he felt a body against his feet.

It was Kelly, face down on the boards. At first Halliday thought he was dead. He got down beside him and felt for his wrist. His pulse was slow, but it was undeniably beating; and as if the flashlight had roused him Kelly moved. But he was still far away. Halliday, kneeling beside him, was conscious of a cold anger. Because Laura had ignored the blackout Kelly had been alone, and because he had been alone—

"Kelly!" he said desperately. "Kelly! Can you hear me?"

"Huh?"

"What happened, Kelly? Who hit you?"

Kelly tried to sit up, but fell back against Halliday's arm.

"I don't know," he said dully. "Somebody—"

He lapsed again. Halliday got up. He did not know what to do. He could not leave him there to get help. Whoever had done this might come back, might even then be watching him. He got out a handkerchief and made a rough bandage. The bleeding had stopped. But the blackout was over before Kelly became fully conscious. Then he raised up on his elbow and was violently sick.

"The dirty devil," he said feebly.

"Who was it? Did you see him?"

"Fellow getting into a rowboat." He lay back and groaned. "I spoke to him, and he came up the ladder. I didn't see the gun until he was right on me."

Halliday looked out over the water, now reflecting the lights of many windows. Why would a man with a rowboat try to kill Kelly? It was queer. It was more than that. Then suddenly, in this new illumination, he saw the rowboat itself. It was under the stern of the ship out in the river. It was hardly more than a shadow, but it was there. And as he looked it began to move downstream, as if it had been pushed out into the current and allowed to drift. He looked at Kelly, slowly getting to his feet.

"There's a boat out there," he said. "Only I can't see anyone in it. Can you get up?"

He got Kelly to his feet. He staggered, but he managed to stand erect. Halliday steadied him.

"That's the boat," he said thickly. "And what the hell do you mean it's empty? He's in it, lying down, maybe with a tarp over him. The murdering devil," he added bitterly.

"He may have been one of the crew, late and getting aboard."

"So he tries to kill me!"

"All right. What?"

"How do I know? Time bomb on the rudder maybe. Something dirty, anyhow." He stiffened. "What did I tell you? He's there. Can't you see him? He's done his job. Now he's getting away with it."

There was a man in the boat now. He was sitting up, rowing furiously downstream, and all at once something was happening to Halliday. It had happened the time he got the medal and the machine gun bullet in his leg. He felt cool and angry and incredibly strong. Adrenalin, probably. He was pouring out adrenalin, only of course he didn't call it that.

"No, by God," he said. "He's not getting away with it. I'll get him if I have to follow him to hell to do it." He looked at Kelly, white and drawn. "Look here, can you get back to the post?"

"I can damn well try."

"All right. Call the river police. Get the other

110

police too. I'll be down along the bank some-where. He'll have to pull in sooner or later."

The boat was well down the stream by now, and out on the water the ship had come to life. It was still dark, but he could see the dim figures of men moving about, and hear the clank and rattle of the chains as the anchors lifted out of the river mud. And he had been right. The man was heading toward the shore, but not sharply. The tide was too strong for that.

He took his automatic out of its holster and put it in the pocket of his trench coat. Then he was out on the street and running. But he knew his first despair then. The street was empty, and along the river side stretched block after block of piers, closed and locked. He could not even see the water. He was in a dead world, blank and empty. But the boat would have to come in somewhere. The man in it would have to land.

He kept on running. The automatic banged against his side, and his bad leg began to weaken. He was gasping for breath, too. But he pounded on, the blood roaring in his ears, sweat pouring down his forehead and into his eyes.

Then he saw it, an open slip; the railway wharf, with a dozen freight cars on it.

The man in the boat had seen it too. He was rowing toward it, coming stealthily as though his oars were muffled; and when he reached it only the faint grating of wood against piling showed that he was there at all. He did not wait to tie the boat. Apparently he gave it a shove and let it go, for it drifted along, bumping until the current caught it. And so cautiously did he climb the ladder that he was on the wharf before Halliday saw him.

He was a big man, and he did not even trouble to look back at the ship, now slowly moving down the river. He came on, and he even stopped in the shadow of a freight car to light a cigarette. Afterwards, looking back, Halliday thought that this casual gesture was what had steadied him. He was no longer gasping. His leg had ceased to hurt. He was entirely calm as he stepped forward and threw his flashlight on the brutal face.

"Just a minute," he said quietly. "I'd like to talk to you."

"What about?"

"What were you doing at that ship?"

"What ship? And take that flashlight away. I don't like it."

The tone was ugly. Halliday had his automatic by that time, but he was just too late. Something exploded in his face, and his helmet, strap and all, was jerked from his head. And with the helmet disappeared forever the mild, patient Halliday who had been a law-abiding citizen, according to his lights, who had paid his taxes, nursed a dying business, and endured his wife patiently for years on end. Now he was a cool fighting devil.

There was no one to see that epic struggle. He never remembered much of it himself. Evidently the man did not want to shoot again, for fear of raising an alarm. He came at Halliday and by sheer force of weight knocked him down and sent his automatic flying. But this new Halliday was up

112

again in a second. Cool does it. Don't let him throw you in the river. Try for his jaw. Get his wind pipe. He's soft. He's big but he's soft. Hit him in the stomach. Where in God's name is the gun? It fell near here. If I can't get it —

The other man was gasping for breath. Fat, Halliday thought. Too much beer. He himself was feeling fine. He wasn't going into the river. He was going to lay out this unprintable mess of foreign jelly, and then he was going to kill him.

It shocked him when he hit the wharf. The man was dodging toward the street, and Halliday was flat on his back. Only he was lying on something. It was his gun, and he fired six shots from it before he saw the man fall. Then he got painfully to his feet.

He reached home that night at half past twelve. A captain of police had shaken him by the hand. A troopship had been saved. And Kelly, being treated for concussion in a hospital, had given him a grin and a final accolade.

'Can't tell about you quiet fellows," he said, "but I knew you were pretty much of a man, Mr. Halliday."

He felt very tired. When he got out of the taxi he was limping badly, and he was carrying a bundle in his arms.

The elevator boy, after a glance at it, chose to ignore it.

"Pretty fine show you folks put on tonight," he said. "Fire engines and ambulances, and just when we thought it was over along came the river police. Guess this town can take care of itself."

113

"Yes," Halliday said drily. "I guess it can."

He took out his key and, unlocking the apartment door, carried the bundle back to his room and put it on the bed. Then still limping he went forward to the living room. The women had gone, and Laura was tucking some bills in her bag and looking complacent.

"Sorry about the windows, Jim," she said. "I had just bid a slam. Have a good time?"

He looked at her, at her new wrist watch, at her carefully manicured hands, at her slightly amused smile, and suddenly he wanted to jar her out of her complacency, to jolt her into a realization that there was a war, and that it was here, at their very doorstep.

"I had to kill a man tonight," he said slowly.

"Really!" said Laura. "What fun!"

She did not believe him. The war for her was still a make-believe, like the test blackout that night. He got up stiffly and went back to his room. The bundle still lay on the bed. He sat down and rubbed his leg, which still ached damnably. He was bruised all over, too, and one of his knuckles was split wide open. They had put a dressing on it at the hospital, but it still hurt like the devil.

He took off his helmet and eyed it. The strap was broken, and there was a fresh dent in the steel. He put it on top of his chiffonier. Then he went to the bundle on the bed. It was stirring. A pair of sleepy eyes looked up at him.

"I sat and sat in the hall," said a small voice. "But nobody came."

"I came, didn't I?"

"Did you?"

"Sure I did."

The boy—Kelly's boy—slept again and Halliday went back to his chair. He knew now what he meant to do. If Kelly wanted to enlist he would keep this child for him. He and Laura. Then when the war was over they would go somewhere out in the country and start again. He would like to grow things. There was always the good green earth, and maybe the boy would spend his vacations with them.

He felt happier than he had felt for a long time. He yawned, and looked at his watch. Then he heard Laura coming back. He smiled rather grimly as he waited for her.

The Portrait

The Portrait

Henrietta Stafford sat at the head of her long table. Her lawyer, a youngish man, sat at the foot. He knew there was no mistake about that. Wherever Henrietta sat was the head of any table. Not that he called her Henrietta, of course.

He looked across the flowers at her erect body and composed face. It was a hard face, he thought, hard and proud. He tried to think of her as she might have been forty or more years ago, when as a widow she first put on the black she had worn ever since. But he could not do it. She looked as though at some time in her life she had frozen into the mould he saw.

She never smiles, he thought. That's what makes her so alarming.

It had been an excellent dinner. All her dinners were like that. He wondered idly how she managed it in times like this. He even ventured to comment on it as the meal ended.

"I see you still have a good cook," he said. "I

don't often get food like this. Do you have any trouble about rationing?"

"You will have to ask Mosely about that, Mr. Negley," she said indifferently. "He does the buying. As for the cook, she is a new one. I pay her a fortune. She should be good."

But he did not ask Mosely. The old man was standing behind her chair, waiting to draw it out, and there was a strange expression on his face. Negley thought he looked frightened. The next moment, however, Henrietta was on her feet, sweeping ahead of him into the library, and Negley was longing for the cigarette he never smoked in her presence.

He knew the library well. It was a handsome room, panelled in dark wood, and over the mantel the portrait in oil of her only son, John. Years ago his senior partner, Forbes, had warned him about the portrait.

"Don't speak to her about it," he had said. "She hasn't mentioned his name to my knowledge since he went to France in the last war. He never came back, poor fellow."

"That's a long time to cherish a grief."

"Grief or remorse. Maybe resentment. I don't know. He married some girl or other shortly before he sailed. She never forgave him."

"Even after he was killed?"

Mr. Forbes had shrugged.

"It was too late then. She wouldn't see the girl, or have anything to do with her."

120

Negley had been curious, but that was all the other man knew. The girl had lived near the camp where John Stafford had trained. "Somewhere in the Middle West," he said. "Came of pretty ordinary people, I imagine. That was the trouble."

"What happened to her?"

"She's dead, I believe. There was a boy. I don't know what became of him. I tried once to speak to Henrietta about him"—he too called her Henrietta behind her back—"but once was enough. She nearly threw me out of the house."

So now he did not glance at the portrait, and whatever had been wrong with Mosely, he was calm enough when he served the coffee. Like everything else it was superlative, and Negley settled down in his chair. So far it had been the usual evening for him. There was nothing to warn him that the woman across from him, looking up at her son's portrait, was about to explode a small bombshell.

"Well," he said, "I gather something has come up, Mrs. Stafford? Is it about your taxes?"

"Once the government has got its hand in my pocket I dare say it is impossible to get it out," she said drily. "No. It is not about taxes, Mr. Negley."

She stopped there. Mosely had come back for the coffee cups, and once more the old look was on his face. He stopped at the door and half-turned, as though he was about say something.

121

He did not, however. He went out and closed the door. Henrietta was not looking at the portrait now. She was sitting still, her veined hands folded tight in her lap, her full black skirts spread about her, her pearls gleaming in the light.

"It is not about taxes," she repeated. "Do you know how old I am, Mr. Negley?" She did not expect an answer. "I am almost seventy, and when a woman has lived as long as that she has no friends. The old ones are dead, and the young ones are not interested." She hesitated, as though it was an effort to go on. "I sent for you because I need help."

Negley was surprised. He sat up and looked at her.

"Help?" he said. "Of course, Mrs. Stafford. Anything I can do—"

She had difficulty in going on. She looked up at the portrait, while Negley waited. Then she said abruptly:

"I have recently learned that my grandson has been killed in the war. He was married shortly before he went abroad. I want to locate his wife."

Perhaps he had been underrating her after all, he thought. Well, why shouldn't she do something for the boy's wife? She was incredibly rich.

"Are you sure?" he asked. "About the grandson, I mean. Sometimes men are reported lost when they are really prisoners. What service was he in?"

"Aviation, a sergeant or something. I learned

of his death only today. Apparently he was reported missing two months ago. Four weeks later he was reported dead." She stopped and looked up again at the portrait. "I suppose you know certain things, Mr. Negley. I resented my son's marriage. I never saw his wife. He could have married anybody. *Anybody,*" she repeated. "But he chose a girl I had never heard of. A nobody. Some cheap little chit from a cheap little town. He married shortly before he sailed, and he never came back," she ended flatly.

God damn it, Negley thought, why doesn't she show some feeling, if she's got it? That flat voice of hers—

"I must say this," she went on. "I did not know John's wife had died. I never knew there was a son. I didn't know it until he came here, almost a year ago. Apparently the mother did not want me to know."

Negley had forgotten his need of a cigarette. He was staring at her in astonishment.

"He came here?" he said. "That's rather curious, after all this time."

"He came here because he was his father's son," she said bitterly. "He was going to the war, and he had married only a few weeks before. He had said good-bye to his wife, he told me, but he wanted to feel that I would look after her, if anything happened to him."

"That was natural, wasn't it?"

"Why? He had married her. I hadn't. No

123

money, no future, and married! He wasn't even an officer."

"Plenty of good men are not officers," Negley said drily.

She did not answer. She got up, and Negley, rising when she did, watched her take a small parcel from the drawer of the big desk.

"There is a photograph in it, and a letter," she said. "I want you to look at them both."

Negley opened the package. In a small leather case was the snapshot of a girl. She was smiling, and she looked young and gay. Underneath it was written: "Always think of me like this, Johnny. I shall be waiting for you."

He was deeply touched. The eyes of the picture were brave and steady, the whole pose one of valiant youth. Henerietta was watching him.

"This is the wife?"

"Yes. I think you'd better read the letter."

He disliked doing it. It was not addressed to him. It was addressed to Sergeant John Stafford, Junior, and written in a clear young hand. But under Henrietta's cold gaze he did so.

"Dearest," it said, "how wonderful of your grandmother to have been so kind to you! I can't get over it, and of course I shall get in touch with her if I need to. So don't worry. Never worry about me, only I miss you so dreadfully. All I do is wait, until this war is over and you are home again. Oh Johnny, how much I love you. I—"

He put down the letter. It seemed indecent to read further. He looked at Henrietta's frozen face.

"How did you get these?"

"An officer left them this afternoon. Mosely talked to him. He had tried to find her at the address given on the letter, but she wasn't there. Nobody knew where she had gone. He looked in the telephone directory and saw my name, so he came here."

"I see," Negley said. "And now you want me to locate the wife. Well, that shouldn't be too hard. And at least, according to that letter, you made young Johnny happy before he left. That must be a comfort to you now, Mrs. Stafford."

She was sitting again, her hands with the old-fashioned dinner ring clasped in her lap. It was a moment before she spoke.

"That letter is a lie," she said.

He glanced at her, thinking he had not heard her correctly. She was looking at him defiantly, a spot of color on each cheek.

"I said," she repeated, "that that letter is a lie. I never promised anything. I couldn't even look at him. I told him he was a fool like his father, and when he tried to talk to me about his wife I ordered him out of this house. You needn't look like that, Mr. Negley. I have had twenty-five years of heartbreak. I couldn't bear any more."

Negley did not say anything. He could see the boy standing, probably in this same room; a boy

125

in an ill-fitting uniform. Scared, perhaps, daunted by the big house and the hard old woman who was his grandmother, yet making his plea for the girl he was leaving behind him. And being rejected, going out into the street again, bewildered and hurt. But not telling his wife. Never telling his wife. Writing a lie to make her happier.

He felt a slow anger rising in him. He was afraid to speak, but Henrietta looked relieved, as though the worst was over.

"You will hardly believe it," she said, "but I almost lost Mosely that night. After thirty years! He came into this room and told me he couldn't live in the house with a woman who could do a thing like that. He didn't go, of course," she added grimly. "Who wants an old man today? And how many people want a butler?"

Suddenly Negley loathed her. He tried to pull himself together.

"I'm afraid I don't understand. Are you saying you have had a change of heart? And that now you want to find this girl?"

She stiffened, if that was possible.

"I may be unnatural, as Mosely said. The boy was nothing to me, but he died for his country. I am at least a good American, Mr. Negley."

"And you think that's enough?"

"What else do you expect?" she said sharply. "This boy had ignored me all his life. His mother took good care of that. I could have done every-

126

thing for him, sent him to school and college, raised him as John's son should have been raised. Instead—" She made a small tired gesture. "Give me some credit," she said. "When Mosely gave me the letter I went to that address. It was a cheap boarding house, and the woman there said she had been gone for a month. She had no idea where she was."

Negley glanced again at the letter. It looked as though it had been read over and over. He felt his throat contracting.

"Just what do you intend, in case I find her?"

"I shall give her adequate support. I don't want to see her. Why should I?"

Negley controlled himself and got up.

"It looks rather difficult," he said. "I suppose if everything else fails we can advertise for her."

She looked so horrified that he almost smiled.

"Advertise?" she said. "Advertise! Have you lost your mind?"

"Well," he said reasonably, "you want to find her, don't you? What's so wrong about that?"

"I intend to do my duty. I do not intend to expose my family problems to the world."

Suddenly Negley lost his temper. He got up and looked down at her, so complacent in her pearls, her solid background, and her pride.

"What do you suppose the world cares about you or your problems just now?" he demanded. "It has other things to think about. Boys and men are dying. Women and children are starving.

Have you ever thought about that, Mrs. Stafford? I felt guilty at your table tonight. I've felt damned guilty for you ever since you told me this story. That boy's writing to his wife, tried to show you to her in a decent light. Only you don't care about that, do you? What you really want is to hide this skeleton in your closet. I'll try to find this girl, but I'm damned if I'll do it for you."

She stared at him incredulously.

"I am not accustomed to being spoken to in that manner, Mr. Negley."

But he was completely out of control by that time. He was astonished to find his voice unsteady.

"Then it's time you were," he said roughly. "You have shut yourself away long enough. You've nourished a grudge for twenty-five years, and all that time you've had everything. You've had luxury. You've had money. You've had your butler, because he can't go anywhere else. And in case you might forget your grudge against the world you've had that portrait over the mantel. Only I'm damned if I see how you can bear to look at it."

. He was still savagely angry when he slammed the library door behind him. He stopped on the stairs to light a cigarette, and found that he was shaking. He began to feel ashamed. All this fury about a boy and a girl he had never seen, he thought, and to a woman almost seventy. There had been something in her face as he went out that had been more than shock. It had been surprise. Well, to hell with her. Let her be surprised. Let her see herself as others saw her for once in her life. It would do her good.

Mosely was waiting with his overcoat in the lower hall. Negley looked at him with a wry gri.

"Afraid I lost my temper," he said.

"Yes, sir," said Mosely. "She is not a happy woman, Mr. Negley."

"Who is?" said Negley roughly. "With the whole world shot to pieces. Nobody has a right to be happy. She's made her own life. If she doesn't like it—"

Mosely said nothing. Negley had an idea that he wanted to speak, that there was something on his mind. Whatever it was he evidently decided against it. As he opened the door Negley stopped.

"What about that officer today? He say anything about where he was staying?"

"At the Savoy-Plaza. His name is Jamieson, Captain Jamieson. Quite a nice person, sir."

"So I imagine," Negley said drily. "That's the sort who are doing our fighting for us."

He looked at his watch as he left the house. It was only ten o'clock; not a good time to find any man just home from the war. Nevertheless he decided to try it. He still felt irritated with himself. He had lost his temper, and he had certainly lost a good client. And for what? Because of a girl's brave eyes and a boy who had written a lie about the old woman who had disowned him. Out in the cold of the winter night he wondered what had happened to him. He was not usually sentimental. Perhaps it was because the war was being fought without him. Young Johnny Stafford had at least had his chance, but nobody wanted a middle-aged lawyer except behind a desk.

To his surprise he found Captain Jamieson in his room. He was in a dressing gown and slippers, a tall rangy young man who looked older than he probably was. He had apparently been lying down, and Negley apologized.

"It's all right," Jamieson said. "Come in and sit down. I'm sorry about the bed. I'm catching up on my sleep."

Negley introduced himself and sat down. He felt awkward. He offered the other man a cigarette and took one himself.

"I thought you might be out. You're just back, aren't you?"

Jamieson nodded.

"I've done the requisite number of jobs. I'm to do some instructing now. It will be a change."

He smiled. He had an attractive smile.

"Had some bad times over there, I imagine," Negley said tentatively.

But Jamieson did not want to discuss the war.

"A bit rugged now and then, of course," he said. "I suppose you want to know about Johnny. He was the hell of a good kid. I'm sorry."

"Then there's no hope? That he's a prisoner, or something like that?"

Jamieson shook his head.

"Not after all this time," he said. "He was on a mission, and the plane must have got lost. The last we heard it was out of gas somewhere over the North Sea. There were ten good men in it. Well, that's war."

He yawned, and Negley got up.

"I wondered about the stuff you brought," he said. "I thought the service took care of things like that."

"They do, but this picture was something special. He always carried it. You know, a sort of mascot. Only that day he didn't. There wasn't time to get it. The letter kind of puzzled me. It had got slipped into the case somehow. He'd never mentioned a grandmother."

"I see," Negley said.

"But he was crazy about his wife. I thought she might like to have the picture, seeing he'd always carried it. I couldn't find her, so I took a chance the grandmother might have the same name. Apparently it worked."

He went on. The British had been fine. Everybody had been fine. But of course it was no dice. He would like to have seen Johnny's wife, to tell her what a good soldier he was. He'd been due for a decoration, too. She would like that. But he yawned again, and Negley finally left.

Outside the hotel he found it was after eleven

o'clock, but he knew it was no use to go home and try to sleep. He decided to go to the address the girl had written in her letter, and he took a taxi there. It was on the West Side, a tall dingy house, but there was a light in the basement and he rang the bell. A sharp-eyed woman opened the door. She looked at him suspiciously.

"I'm inquiring about a Mrs. John Stafford," he said. "I believe she lived here at one time."

"So you're after her too!" she said. "What's she done? What's all the excitement about? First an officer in a uniform asks for her. Then a hard-faced old woman in a mink coat. And now you."

"I thought you might tell me something about her."

"Just what I told the others, mister. She just walked out the day she got word her husband was dead, and never came back. Owing me two weeks' rent too."

Negley reached for his wallet, but she shook her head.

"The old lady took care of that," she said. "You'd better come inside. It's cold."

He went in. The hall was dingy but clean. Nevertheless it was strange to compare it to Henrietta's, its marble floor, its old French consoles and mirrors. The woman seemed glad to talk.

"She was a nice girl," she said. "They hadn't been married long, and they were crazy about each other. When he was moved near here she came East too. She got a job in a war plant, and

132

she was doing all right. Only when the word came he was missing she gave it up. Funny thing, mister, she kept saying he was alive, that she would know if he was dead. Then this letter came from the War Department, and she just walked out."

"What about her things?" Negley said, puzzled. "Did she take them with her?"

"That's what worried me. I didn't tell that snooty old girl this afternoon, but they're still here. She didn't take nothing, and that's a month ago."

Negley did not sleep much that night. He was afraid there might be another sin on Henrietta's proud old soul. It was useless to remind himself that all over the world women were standing up to just such catastrophes. This girl was young, too young to have learned fortitude. There had been courage in that picture of her. It had been a brave young face, determinedly smiling, but it might be the courage which it took to leap off a bridge, or to end a life somehow.

He had learned other things from the woman where she had lived.

"She gave up her job for fear some word would come about him and she wouldn't be here. She never left the house after that. She just sat and waited. She didn't even eat."

He wakened early the next morning. Some of the night's anxiety had gone, and he felt rather sheepish when he called the Morgue. Nevertheless he was relieved when he was told that nobody answering the girl's description had been brought in during the last month. But he had reached a dead end. She seemed to have had no family, no roots anywhere. He didn't even know from what town she had come, or where she had been working.

He saw his partner that morning before he went to his own office.

"I'm afraid I lost us a client last night," he said.

"Not Henrietta!"

"Henrietta. I told her some unpleasant facts. She didn't like them."

Mr. Forbes grunted.

"I suppose it was coming to her," he said resignedly. "How'd it happen?"

Negley told him, feeling rather like a bad boy as he did so. But Forbes was philosophic.

"She may get over it," he said. "She's not a bad sort, gives a lot to charity and all that. Of course she gets it deducted from her income tax." He grinned wryly. "We'd better try the Bureau of Missing Persons," he said. "At least that won't get Henrietta in the papers, and I'd like to find that girl. If she's to be found," he added.

It was a busy day. No word came from the Stafford house. Evidently Henrietta was still nursing her wrath. Negley had called the Bureau of Missing Persons, and an investigator had come around. He seemed disappointed at the lack of information, but he was a cheerful soul.

"We generally find them," he said. "You'd be surprised how hard it is to lose yourself these days."

At least he had done all he could, Negley thought. He went through the rest of the day's routine as usual, and he was signing his mail late in the afternoon when Mosely was announced. When he came in he looked profoundly shaken. He stood in front of the desk, fingering a shabby hat. Negley remembered that he had never seen him in ordinary clothing before.

"What's wrong, Mosely?" he asked. "Anything new?"

Mosely's face twitched.

"I thought I'd better tell you, Mr. Negley," he said. "Mrs. Stafford has dismissed me."

Negley put down his pen.

"I don't believe it."

"It's true, sir. I'm out of a job, after thirty years."

Negley swore under his breath.

"Sit down," he said. "Sit down and tell me about it. What happened? Why did she do it? Was it because I—?

Mosely sat down, putting his hat carefully on the floor beside him.

"No, sir," he said. "It's nothing to do with you." He cleared his throat. "I believe the technical charge is theft, sir."

"Theft!"

Mosely attempted a smile.

"I've been an honest man all my life. I've served Mrs. Stafford well for a long time. I've been her friend. Sometimes I've thought I was her only friend. When her boy was killed years ago she cried on my shoulder."

Negley squared himself in his chair.

"But theft, Mosely. What do you mean?"

Mosely looked embarrassed.

"It's true, in a way. It wasn't much. A little here and there for the last few weeks. But we have a new cook. The old one would have understood. You see, she's been very sick, sir. She needed the little extra I couldn't give her."

"What are you talking about?" Negley asked impatiently. "Who's been sick? The old cook?"

Mosely was shocked.

"Oh no, sir, I thought I told you. I'm a little nervous, I guess. It's Mr. Johnny's wife."

It was a moment before Negley could speak. Then he got up and going around his desk put a hand on the man's shaking shoulder.

"You're a better man than I am, Mosely," he said gravely. "I only talk. You act. So you've got her. Good God, why didn't you say so before? I've been going through hell all day."

Mosely was apologetic.

"I wanted to tell you last night," he said, "but I was afraid. You might have gone back and told Mrs. Stafford, and I didn't know how she would take it."

136

"She's going to take it and like it," said Negley grimly.

The story, when he got it, was brief. The girl, Mrs. Johnny as Mosely called her, had come to the house when she received the word her husband was dead. "She seemed to think Mrs. Stafford would want to see her." But she had fainted in the lower hall, and when she came out of it he had not known what to do. In the end he called a taxicab and took her to his sister, who had a small apartment in the Bronx. She was a semi-invalid, and Mosely supported her.

"The girl was delirious that first night," Mosely said. "She kept calling for Johnny, and we couldn't quiet her. She's been sick ever since, but she's better now. My sister is elderly, but she took good care of her. Only of course we couldn't afford the things she needed, so — well, I told her Mrs. Stafford had sent them."

His voice trailed off. There as a moment's silence. Negley broke it.

"Why on earth haven't you told Mrs. Stafford?" he asked impatiently. "At least she's a just woman."

"She had no love for this girl," Mosely said simply, "and that's what she needed."

Well, it was as good an answer as any, Negley thought. Perhaps that was what the world needed, more love, and less hard justice. He shoved his mail to one side and got his hat.

"I want to see her," he said. "Maybe I won't

give her love, but you can be sure she's going to get what's coming to her. And you're not going to suffer, either."

His face felt stiff as he left the office with Mosely that afternoon. It still felt stiff with indignation when, at nine o'clock that night, he rang the Stafford doorbell. He was remembering a thin bit of a hollow-eyed girl who had smiled at him wanly from her bed.

"Please thank Johnny's grandmother for being so kind to me," she said. "Johnny would be pleased."

She had not cried. She had simply lain back among her pillows, alive but not caring.

"I'll get up soon," she said. "I don't want to be a burden to her."

The parlormaid let him in, and he stalked rigidly up the stairs. This was the showdown. He didn't care if he never saw Henrietta Stafford again. He didn't care if they lost her business. He didn't care if she threw him out of the house. But he was aware as he entered the room that something in it was changed. Not Henrietta, sitting stiffly in her chair behind the coffee tray. Not the furniture. And then he saw it. The portrait was gone from over the mantel.

It threw him off step, so to speak. He started at the landscape which had replaced it, but Henrietta did not mention it. She eyed him coolly.

"If you have come about Mosely," she said, "it is entirely useless."

138

"I haven't come about Mosely."

"Then perhaps you will explain this unexpected visit."

"I'll be glad to," he said. "I'll be damned glad to, as a matter of fact." For the first time in that room—or in that house—he took out a cigarette and lit it. She did not say anything. "I've come to tell you you are going to take Mosely back, and that I think you ought to get down on your knees and beg his pardon. What he took from you, Mrs. Stafford, went to feed your grandson's wife. He has nursed and cared for her. And when I asked him why he didn't tell you about her, what do you think he said?"

She still said nothing.

"He said she needed love, and he didn't trust you for that. So he hid her."

Then at last she flushed. Out of habit she looked up for the portrait, but it as gone. She looked at Negley.

"Those are hard words, Mr. Negley."

"They're true, aren't they?"

It was some time before she spoke. Some of the rigidity had gone out of her as she sat. She looked old and rather pathetic. But she was still Henrietta.

"I am too old to change," she said. "Don't ask too much of me. I don't know this girl. I can't promise to love her. But I will look after her. And I will apologize to Mosely. I didn't know of course, but I want him back. I need him and I—

am fond of him."

He was quite sure there were tears in her eyes when he left.

He walked home that night. He had done his best. He had not changed Henrietta, but at least the portrait was gone. Now at last she was on her own, with no painted image to nourish her bitter memories. And perhaps—who could tell?—she might care for Johnny's wife some day. He had an idea that she needed someone to care for.

He had undressed and was looking over a magazine when his telephone rang. He hardly recognized the voice as Henrietta's. There was something new in it, something he had not heard before. It was, he thought, almost human, although it had lost none of its dignity.

"I am sorry if I have disturbed you," she said, "but Mosely has just shown me a picture in the newspaper tonight. It is of some men picked up at sea by a tanker and taken to Murmansk. Mosely thinks one of them is John's boy. It's possible. It looks very much like him."

"Certainly I hope so," Negley said. "It's great news if it is."

She seemed to hesitate.

"I am calling the War Department now," she said. "I know some men there. If it is true I would like to be the one to tell his wife."

Perhaps miracles did happen, after all. He was a trifle dazed as he put down the receiver. He felt sure that the boy would be Johnny, and he thought vaguely that there must be a Power somewhere which did things in its own way. It took care of reckless boys and old men like Mosely, and even of lovers, although sometimes it separated them to meet, perhaps later, in some young and thrilling heaven of its own.

He even thought that it took care of the Henrietta of this world and saved them from themselves. And after his own fashion he muttered what — in spite of its words — amounted to a prayer as he crawled into bed that night.

"Well, I'll be eternally God-damned," he said.

Alibi for Isabel

Alibi for Isabel

Sally always felt better in church after the general confession. It gave her a sort of moral support, as though it said that not only she, Sally Fielding, had committed a sin; but that all other men and women were sinners. The remission too was comforting. It promised forgiveness in exchange for repentance, and Sally had been faithfully repenting for the last twelve years.

She rose slowly from her knees. The hassock had been small and hard, and her knees hurt a little. As usual she sat down on her purse, and the children giggled. Scott put out a hand to quiet them, and she glanced at him. Looking at him had somewhat the same effect on her as had the service. He gave her the same sense of safety. But there was something wrong with him just then. His face had set, suddenly, as though something had shocked him.

She watched him furtively through the sermon. He did not relax, she thought. He sat staring forward as though he did not dare to turn his head. The children wriggled and squirmed, but he paid no attention. Then, during the Te Deum, she glanced around the neighboring pews, and she saw Isabel. It was certainly Isabel, Isabel in a gay red hat, looking sober and devout. But Isabel just the same. Sally swayed and caught the back of the pew in front of her. Only that held her upright. She felt as though her heart had stopped.

When she sat down Anne was whispering to her.

"Daddy looks funny, doesn't he?"

"Hush, Anne. Don't talk."

Her brain was whirling. After twelve years, she thought desperately. Twelve years of building a life with Scott, of bearing the children, of good deeds and repentance, and now the past had caught up with her. She never doubted that. Why else was Isabel there in this small suburban church, fifty miles from where she belonged? And Isabel, slightly behind her and to the right, was watching her. She could feel her eyes on her, interested and calculating.

She did not want to go out when the service ended. She straightened Anne's hat and found Johnny's cap on the floor. Scott was waiting patiently in the aisle. She had to pass him, and as she did so she felt his hand on her shoulder.

"Forget it," he said in a low voice. "Why on earth should she scare you?"

She braced herself and tried to stop trembling. "What's she doing here?" she asked.

There was no answer, of course, and to her relief the red hat was already near the church door. Perhaps it was coincidence after all. The rector in his cassock greeted them with a smile.

"How is my favorite family?" he said cheerily. "And how's the Victory garden?"

Scott said something, but Sally could give him only a faint smile. Isabel was waiting on the walk outside, a tall showy woman with bold eyes and slightly faded blonde hair. She did not look ominous. She was merely waiting, casual and poised. She had always been very sure of herself. Sally felt Scott grip her arm.

"Steady, old girl," he said. "She probably lives somewhere around here, or she's visiting someone. Why should she worry you?"

That gave her a little courage. If Scott was only afraid that there might be a revival of the old story about Terry, at least it showed that he had no suspicion of the truth. It even enabled her to look surprised when Isabel greeted her.

"Hello, Sally," she said. "Don't tell me these kids are yours!"

"Of course they are. Scott, you remember Isabel Worthing, don't you?"

"Isabel Eaton, now," Isabel corrected her. "I married Jim Eaton years ago. Or maybe it only seems like that. When his mother died he took a yen for the old place. God knows why."

So Isabel was living in the old Eaton house outside of town, Sally's heart missed another beat.

"It bores me stiff," Isabel said. "Let me come in and see you sometime, Sally. We can talk over old times."

Sally repressed a shudder.

"Of course. Do you know where we live?"

"Know where the outstanding citizens of the community live? The leading exponents of family life! My dear, how could I help it?"

It was innocuous, of course. Isabel under her red hat, smiling, and Sally feeling as though she had been impaled like a butterfly on a pin. For now she was certain Isabel had come to church deliberately, for some purpose of her own. What was she going to do, after all these years? What could she do?

She was trembling when she got into the car beside Scott, and he reached over and put a hand on her knee.

"Stop it, darling," he said. "She's not a bad sort. After all she was a good friend when you needed one, and if she's married to Jim Eaton I'm sorry for her."

He was starting the car. He did not see her white despairing face.

"I'm afraid she means to make trouble," she said. "What she said about old times—"

"Nonsense," he said gruffly. "That's all water over the dam. What happened to you has happened to a lot of women. If she's a nuisance throw her out."

As easy as that, she thought. Just throw Isabel out and forget her. If only she had told Scott the truth before she married him she might have done just that. But she hadn't. She had tried after he proposed to her.

"There's something you ought to know, Scott. It's about Terry."

He had looked impatient.

"Can't you forget Terry? I'm not marrying his widow. I'm marrying you."

She had persisted.

"I'll feel better if I talk about it."

"Well, I won't." He had held her off and looked at her. "Unless," he said gravely, "you can't forget him. If you still care about him, or his memory—"

"Oh, no. Never," she gasped. "How could I, Scott? I don't think I ever loved him. Not really."

So she had never told him, and now here was Isabel, threatening all she had so carefully built—her home, her family, the husband who was all he should have been. She looked at him, his handsome face, his tall strong body, the heavy hair slightly gray over the ears, and she knew that no price was too great to keep him.

149

At the house Scott put the car in the garage while she took the children into the house. It was cool and neat, and the hall was filled with the odor of frying chicken. The children sniffed excitedly.

"Chicken and ice cream," they chanted. "Chicken and ice cream."

They ran for the funny papers, and Sally looked around her house. Everything had changed, yet everything was the same. In the dining room Gracie, the second maid, was putting a bowl of peonies in the exact center of the table. She looked concernedly at Sally.

"Don't you feel well, Mrs. Fielding?"

"I'm all right. Why, Gracie?"

"You look sort of pale. Maybe it's the heat."

"Yes, it is warm."

Perhaps it was all right after all. Outside Scott was whistling on his way in from the garage, and the children were reading the funnies with their usual sobriety. Queer, how they never laughed over them. It might have been any Sunday, as it had been for years and years. Or as Isabel had said, maybe it only seemed like that. Isabel again! She must put her out of her mind or she would go crazy.

She managed to get through the meal, and the day followed its usual course. Scott put on a pair of overalls and went out to work in the vegetable garden at the back of the house. Anne

150

took her doll for a walk, and little Johnny took a nap and got up to run around the lawn, firing a wooden machinegun at all and sundry. Sally took her knitting onto the shady porch, but she did not knit. She merely waited. She knew that from now on she would always be waiting, until Isabel came and she knew the worst.

It was Tuesday before she came, and it caught her unawares, at that. It was Gracie's day to help the laundress, and Mrs. Ward, the cook, would not take a step beyond the pantry door. Sally was carrying out the lunch dishes when she heard someone in the hall.

"Hello!" said Isabel's voice. "Where are you?"

Sally almost dropped the tray. She put it down and drew a long breath.

"I'm here," she said. "Wait a minute. I'm coming."

Isabel however did not wait. She sauntered into the living room, cool and nonchalant, and looked around her. Sally noticed that she wore a scarf around her neck.

"Very domestic, aren't you?" she said. "I always knew you would have a room like this, chintz and flowers and so on. It looks like you." She lit a cigarette and sat down. "I gather it's a success. Your second marriage, I mean."

"I'm very happy, Isabel."

If there was appeal in her voice Isabel did not notice it.

"I suppose there's a law of some sort. You get so much misery and so much happiness out of life. Only it seems to have missed me."

"Missed you? Is something wrong?"

Isabel laughed.

"That's putting it mildly," she said drily. "I'm married to a drunken beast who is trying to get rid of me. And he doesn't care how."

So it wasn't going to be bad after all. Isabel was not inimical. She was merely unhappy. Sally relaxed.

"I'm dreadfully sorry, Isabel. You deserve something better than that."

Isabel however was not asking for pity.

"It's a good thing I'm stronger than he is." She touched the scarf at her throat. "He has an idea when he's drinking that the best way to get rid of me is to choke me to death. So far I've been lucky."

Sally gasped.

"Why on earth don't you leave him?" she asked.

Isabel shook her head.

"I'm not giving him that satisfaction. And I'm not joining the alimony squad just yet. He's a drunken sadist. I thought I knew my way about, but I didn't know there were such people. He killed my canary last night. That's what we fought about."

Sally looked incredulous.

"He must be insane, Isabel. Like—like Terry."

Isabel laughed.

"Try to get him committed! It isn't crazy to choke your wife and kill birds. Not in the courts anyhow."

She changed the subject abruptly.

"That's enough about me," she said. "Let's hear about you. I suppose it was worth while, wasn't it?"

Sally stiffened. So it was coming after all.

"I'll never forget how you looked," Isabel went on. "To tell the truth I didn't think you had it in you. You were such a mild little thing. It was funny, too. You couldn't even scream. I had to do it for you."

"Do we have to talk about it?"

"Why not?" said Isabel carelessly. "It was my one good deed, like the Scouts. Maybe I like to remember it."

Sally was quiet now, with the stillness of desperation.

"Just what is all this about, Isabel?" she said. "You're not merely making a call. You're trying to do something to me. If you're trying to make me wretched, you are. If you mean to break up my home—"

Isabel raised her eyebrows.

"Break up your home when I helped you get it? Why should I? Can't we talk about the past? It's over. What harm in that?" She looked about

153

the room again. "I can't say I don't envy you. You've got everything; even a couple of kids. Maybe I'm just envious."

But she let it go at that, and she left soon after, driving away in her smart coupé, and waving to Sally as she started. Sally went back into the house and stopped in front of the hall mirror. What she saw was a pale young woman in a blue house dress with a smudge on her nose and a small set face. For she was not fooled. She knew now that some day Isabel meant to come back, and that when she did she would wipe away her marriage and all it stood for with one sweep of her large white hands.

Automatically she called Johnny in from the swing in the grounds and took him upstairs for his nap. As she undressed him the feel of his small wriggling body on her knee brought tears to her eyes. He saw that and reached for her face.

"You crying, Mummy?"

"No, darling. It's all right."

He was satisfied. She put him in his bed and drew the sheet over him.

"When I grow up I'm going to be a soldier," he said, already drowsy.

"That's fine. Be a good soldier, Johnny."

"Is Daddy a soldier?"

"He was, a long time ago."

She left him and going into her own room

closed and locked the door. A soldier, she thought. Terry had been one too in the last war, only it had done something to his mind. She hadn't known that until she married him. He had fooled everybody, including herself. But he was not bad until the time he tried to kill them both with his old service automatic. He had even written a double suicide note.

"Here's something I want you to sign, Sally."

"What is it, Terry?"

"Never mind about that. Just sign it."

She had read it, however, and almost fainted. Then she refused, until he held the gun to her head. She signed, because she had to, but she knew he meant it. So she had got the gun from him, and as he came at her to take it she shot him instead. Only Isabel had lived in the apartment across the hall, and the door was not locked. Sally was standing in the living room, still holding the gun, when she walked in.

"What goes on?" she said. Then she saw Terry on the floor. She did not gasp or even change color. She bent over the body and then stood up. "I suppose you had your reasons," she said coolly. "Only—isn't this rather extreme?"

Sally heard her own voice. She had not known she had breath to speak.

"He was going to kill us both. He made me sign that note."

Isabel walked over to the desk by the window

155

and picked up the note. Apparently nobody had heard the shot, for the building was quiet. Sally was still holding the gun, but she did not look at Terry, lying there on the floor. Isabel read the note slowly.

"Crazy," she said. "Crazy as a June-bug. We'd better get the police."

"The police? But he was going to shoot me. I had to."

She remembered sitting down then, but still not looking at Terry. Everywhere else, but not at Terry.

"I imagine you have a pretty good defense," said Isabel drily. "Anyhow no jury would send you to the chair."

Sally let the gun slide to the floor. Shocked as she was this was the first time she had realized what she had done. It was not that she had loved Terry. She had known from the first days of her marriage that she never had. And that he was strange at times. But she was still very young, only nineteen, and she had done her best to look after him.

She would try to soothe him.

"Go to sleep, Terry dear. I'm here. I'll hold you."

"Keep your hands off me. Let me alone."

It had been like that, and now she had killed him.

Everything had happened so quickly that she

was still dazed. She had been in the kitchenette, getting dinner. She heard Terry come in, and when he did not call to her she knew he was in one of his black moods. Things were pretty bad with them just then, that summer of 1932, but she was trying to manage. She went into the living room to put out the gate-legged table, and he was writing at the desk by a window. She hadn't seen the gun. He must have had it in front of him.

"I'll have dinner ready in a minute," she said. "What are you writing?"

That was when he got up and ordered her to sign.

She hadn't meant to kill him. Isabel knew that. She had got the gun and because he was coming at her with murder in his face she fired it. She had had to stop him somehow. That was all she had thought. She had had to stop him.

She didn't know whether Isabel believed her or not that day. She didn't say anything. She stooped down and picked up the gun, and stood looking at it. Then quite deliberately she wiped it with her handkerchief.

"No man's worth dying for," she said. "Or even going to the pen. He killed himself. He's threatened to, hasn't he?"

Sally nodded mutely, and Isabel stooped swiftly and pressed Terry's still warm fingers on the weapon. After that she let it drop on the floor beside him and when she straightened she looked at Sally.

"How loud can you scream?" she inquired.

It had been as simple as that. When people came hurrying to the apartment they found Sally in her bedroom crying hysterically, and Terry apparently a suicide on the floor. Isabel managed everything, even to the scream. Only this was queer. When the police came there was no suicide note, not even the one she had signed. The coroner spoke of it at the inquest.

"It is usual for individuals about to take their lives to leave some written indication of their purpose. However, this is not invariable. People differ, and in this case the deceased was known to be mentally unstable and at times depressed."

The verdict had been suicide, and Scott Fielding had taken Sally home that day. He had known Terry.

"I want to say something," he told her in the taxi, "but I find it rather hard. Terry was shell-shocked during the war. I don't think he ever got over it. What he did was a part of that. Don't ever blame yourself."

She had wanted to tell then, only the taxi had stopped and she had had to get out. She had gone up to the apartment, where someone had washed the carpet, and the superintendent's wife had packed Terry's clothes in his trunk. But that reference of the coroner's to a suicide note had frightened her. If two people sign such a statement and only one dies, wasn't that suspicious? She didn't know. She felt caught in a maze of lies and deception. And she couldn't find the note anywhere.

She was crying heartbrokenly when Isabel came in that night. Isabel had a good secretarial job. Perhaps it had made her practical. She eyed her with disapproval.

"Now look," she said. "What's done is done. You won't help it by crying your eyes out. Have you had anything to eat today?"

Sally shook her head.

"I'll make some coffee, and a poached egg won't hurt you. Now go in and wash your face in cold water, and stop this nonsense."

She was sick for a long time after that. During the day the superintendent's wife looked after her, and Isabel took over at night. She had to get well, of course. There was almost no money. Then one evening Scott Fielding heard she had been ill and came to see her. She was sitting up in a chair by that time, and he looked worried when he saw how thin she was.

"I don't know," he said, "or I'd have been here before this. Why didn't someone let me know?"

After that he came often. He practiced law, it developed, in a town fifty miles from the city, and it was surprising how frequently business brought him to town. When she found herself

159

falling in love with him she determined to tell him the whole story. She said so to Isabel, only Isabel said she was a little idiot.

"He may believe you, but he'll see blood on your hands just the same," she said.

That was probably why, the next time he came, Isabel wandered in to give him a highly detailed story of Terry's death, of how she had heard the shot and Sally screaming, and had run in to find Terry dead on the floor with the gun beside him.

Scott however had resented it.

"How often does she do that sort of thing?" he demanded after she had gone.

"She's never done it before."

"Well, it's pretty rotten," he said. "I don't think you ought to be exposed to it."

Which was probably why, that same night, he had asked her to marry him.

"I know it's too soon," he said. "I know how much you cared for Terry. But if it's any excuse I'm very deeply in love with you, my dear. Perhaps some day you can care for me."

And she had thrown caution to the winds. What else could she do, after Isabel?

"I care now," she said, her voice shaken. "I care terribly, Scott."

She had had about twelve years. Happy, blissful years. If anything, the relationship between them had grown closer. He was tender and kind, and for all the gray over his ears he had a boyishness she adored. Terry became a dim memory. There were weeks, months—except in church during the confession—when she forgot her tragedy entirely. She had even forgotten the scene with Isabel and Scott until the day a year later when she married him. Before she left for the church Isabel told her why she had done it.

"I guess I fixed him that night," she said complacently. "You're safe. You have nothing to worry about from now on."

Sally was ready to go. She was wearing a soft gray dress and a bunch of orchids, and she had gone to early church to ask forgiveness and that she might make Scott a good wife. But something in Isabel's face stopped her.

"Look, Isabel," she said. "What did you do with the note Terry left? I never found it."

"Burned it," Isabel said promptly. "That thing meant trouble, and don't think it didn't!"

So she married Scott. She felt safe. She had been safe. Only now here was Isabel again. She knew quite well where she stood. To tell Scott now was to tell him she had lived a lie for twelve years. He might believe her. He would probably try to understand. But the old close relationship would be gone. When he was tired, or when he was alone, he would see her shooting Terry and Isabel wiping her fingerprints off the gun. He would be sorry for her. But he would ask why

161

she had not told him. To kill in self-defense was not a crime. No jury she knew now would have convicted her. Yet he had had a right to know, and she had deceived him.

Nevertheless she meant to fight for him, Isabel or no Isabel, so she dressed carefully that night, even using mascara and more than a touch of rouge. Somehow she felt that she must hold him now as she had never tried before. She looked almost like a girl when he came in.

"Well, whose debutante are you?" he inquired gaily.

"Yours, if you want me."

He put his arms around her.

"I always want you, darling," he said. "Always and ever."

But she felt rather like the mermaid in the fairy tale, to whom the witch gave legs so she could leave the sea for her lover; the price being that every step was to be as if she walked on naked swords.

She began to breathe more normally at the end of a week. Isabel was not at church on Sunday, and life began to settle down again. Then on Wednesday, fixing some flowers in the living room, she saw the coupé at the door and Isabel coming up the walk. She wore the red hat, but there was a bit of veiling to shade her eyes, and when she came in Sally saw the reason. Under the veil and make-up Isabel had a badly swollen eye.

She was cold and unsmiling, too. She stalked into the living room and determinedly closed the door to the hall behind her.

"You'll have to help me, Sally," she said. "I've taken all I'm going to."

"Help you? I'll do anything I can, of course, Isabel. What do you want?"

"Do I have to put it into words?" Isabel demanded grimly. "Don't be dumb, Sally. I'm through, and I mean through. Don't argue with me. It's too late for that."

When Sally said nothing she came and stood over her.

"See here," she said. "I saved you once. I saved you a lot of trouble. Maybe worse. You can thank me for what you've got. Now don't you think it's your turn?"

Sally got her breath.

"That was self-defense, Isabel. You know it. Terry meant to kill me."

"What do you think this is?" Isabel demanded, and touched her face. "I tell you he means to finish me."

The house was still, but in Sally's ears there was a roaring like the beating of the sea. She could hardly hear her own voice.

"You can't do a thing like that," she said. "It's wicked. It's horrible. And you'll be suspected at once. Even your servants—"

"I haven't told you what I am going to do."

"You don't need to. You're going to kill your husband."

Isabel lit a cigarette. She seemed to be thinking. She was quieter now, but with the quietness of determination.

"You can't stop it, Sally," she said finally. "Nobody can stop it. And it won't hurt you. I want only one thing from you."

"If you mean a gun—"

"Never mind about that," Isabel said. "All I want from you is an alibi."

"An alibi?" Sally repeated. "I don't understand. How can I—?"

"Of course you understand." Isabel was impatient. "I'll be with you. Who would doubt your word? The respected Sally Fielding, who goes to church on Sunday and works for Red Cross the rest of the week! That's all you have to do. Say I was with you when it happens."

Sally got up. They stood face to face, two antagonists, all pretension thrown aside.

"And suppose I don't?" Sally said. "What about that, Isabel?"

"I think," said Isabel, "that I would have to tell Scott Fielding the real story about Terry."

Sally was fighting now. Her voice was defiant.

"He won't believe you. It would be only your word against mine."

"He might believe the note."

164

So that was it. Isabel still had the note. Sally stood without moving. The roaring in her ears was worse, and she could hardly hear the children, coming in exuberantly and being taken upstairs by Gracie. Isabel listened to them, then she threw away her cigarette and turned to the door.

"Try not to hate me, Sally," she said. "If I had anything like that I might be different. And I'm not asking you to pay a high price for them."

"You're trying to make me into a criminal. That's high enough."

Fortunately Scott did not come home to dinner that night. He had a client from out in the country, and she was in bed when he came upstairs. She pretended to be asleep, and he moved about quietly, not to waken her. He did not even turn on his reading lamp, and this care of her sent burning tears under her eyelids. What price was too high to keep him? And she knew Isabel. She meant to kill Jim Eaton. It would happen, sooner or later, no matter what she did.

She slept very little that night. She could not go to the police. After all there was as yet no crime. She debated telling Scott; after all, risking their life together to save another life which hardly seemed worth saving. Then she wondered if she could warn Jim Eaton himself. She had seen him once or twice, a stocky man with the congested eyes of the steady drinker. But how?

165

She had no idea what Isabel meant to do. He would only laugh at her.

Nevertheless she did try, the next morning. She saw Isabel from a distance in town, while she was doing her own marketing, and she slipped into a drugstore and called the Eaton house from a booth.

She was so shaky that she dropped her money and had to fumble for it on the dirty floor. She got the house however, and asked for Jim Eaton.

"Mr. Eaton is asleep," said a man's voice. The butler's, she thought. "Can I take a message?"

"No. This is very important. Please tell him."

"Who is calling?"

"It doesn't matter. Only I must speak to him. I must."

"Just a moment."

He left the receiver off, and she could hear him moving away. It was hot in the booth and she felt faint. But the voice which finally came back was the butler's again.

"I'm sorry, madam," he said. "Mr. Eaton can't be disturbed."

She was shocked when she opened the door to find Isabel standing there.

"Don't tell me," she said, "that you were trying to warn my beloved husband! I rather thought you might. I saw you coming in."

"You needn't worry. I didn't get him," Sally said dully.

166

Isabel laughed.

"I could have saved you your nickel. He's dead to the world. Only I wouldn't try it again, Sally. He knows anyhow, only he thinks he'll get me first."

That was on Wednesday. Isabel called her on Friday morning.

"How are you off for gas?" she asked. "I can give you a couple of gallons if you need it. I thought we might take a drive this afternoon."

"A drive?"

Isabel sounded irritated.

"What's wrong with that?" she said sharply. "I haven't seen this part of the country at all. I don't know the roads. Of course if you don't want to be seen with me—"

A drive, Sally thought. It sounded innocent enough. Perhaps Isabel merely wanted to try to persuade her again.

"It's not that," she said. "I'd like to show you the country. It's lovely just now. Where will I pick you up?"

"I'll wait for you at our gate at two o'clock. Unless you need the gas. We have some. Black market stuff probably. Jim buys it. I don't."

"I don't need any, thanks."

At least, she thought despairingly, it was a reprieve. She could make another protest, and maybe Isabel would let Scott get her a divorce. After all Jim Eaton was a notorious drunkard.

Scott could get her a decent alimony, and she could go away somewhere. She was almost gay as she dressed after lunch. She put on a white dress and the blue hat that Scott said brought out the color in her eyes, and she saw Isabel eying her when she stopped the car.

"Fine," she said. "Leading citizen's wife takes old friend for drive and tea. Where can we have tea, Sally?"

At Isabel's request they drove through the towns, and at the grocer's she got out and bought some cheese. Only when she was back in the car were Sally's suspicions roused. Isabel dropped the package and lit a cigarette.

"That man will remember me," she said casually. "He saw you too."

"Why does that matter?"

"Think about it," Isabel said drily. "I am out with you. We're taking a drive and having tea somewhere. I've bought cheese for the cold supper the servants leave. Quite domestic, you see. They all go out together on Wednesdays," she added. "It saves gas and bother."

Sally felt the nightmare closing down on her. This was it, then. She was to drive Isabel by some roundabout route to the Eaton place, she would get out and kill her husband, and then they were to go somewhere to tea. Unconsciously she took her foot off the gas.

"Just keep going," Isabel said, her voice not

unkindly. "This has nothing to do with you, Sally. It's between Jim and me." She looked at her wrist watch. "You might step on it," she said. "It's three o'clock. They'll be gone by the this time."

Sally drove on. Isabel knew the roads after all, and by a roundabout route of untraveled back lanes they finally reached the woods behind the Eaton place. There Isabel stopped her.

"I'll get out here," she said. "I've just remembered something. I won't be long."

She disappeared into the woods, and Sally sat still, her hands frozen on the wheel. Somewhere a squirrel was chattering, and over everything was the stillness and peace of the June countryside. So unreal was the situation that as Isabel disappeared into the woods Sally almost called to her that she had forgotten the cheese, sharp and pungent on the seat beside her.

Then she understood. The cheese, like the grocer and herself, was to be a part of Isabel's alibi. She had bought it, but when she came home later she would still be carrying it. She would walk in, as imperturbable as the day she had found Sally standing with the gun over Terry's body, and if the police were there—Sally never doubted that she had arranged for someone else to find Jim—she could say:

"Of course I haven't been back since I left. Ask Mrs. Fielding. And look at this cheese. Do

169

you think I'd have carried it all afternoon if I'd been back?"

What could she do? It was too late to call Scott, or to notify the police. It was too late to do anything. She began to feel faint. Her hands and feet were cold, and the smell of the cheese sickened her. At the end of half an hour Isabel had not returned, and she crawled out of the car and lost her lunch at the edge of the woods. She did not go back to the car. She sat on the ground, thinking that now she was responsible for two deaths, and that she could never go to church again, or face her children. Only she would tell Scott. He would have to know now. Know everything.

It was five o'clock when she got into the car again. Isabel had not returned. She was certain now that she never would. Something had gone wrong, and Jim Eaton had killed her instead. He had tried to before. Now he had done it.

She drove slowly back to town, taking the main road this time and trying to look about her, as though she were seeing it for the last time; the small neat house, the green fields, the playing children. When she got home she did not garage the car. Scott was standing on the porch waiting for her, and he called to her to leave it at the curb.

He came to meet her on the path, and his face was grave.

"I'm afraid I have rather a shock for you, darling," he said. "Jim Eaton's dead."

"I know," she said, and staggered slightly. He put his arm around her.

"I always said he'd kill himself. Now he's done it."

"But he didn't," she gasped. "I must tell you, Scott. Isabel—"

He didn't hear her. He was intent on what he had to tell her.

"I've been out to see her, Sally. She's all right, only shocked, of course. She wasn't with him. He was drunk, and he hit a telephone pole out on the highway and crashed. I thought you might want to go out and see her. After all she's an old friend of yours."

She didn't say anything. All at once she realized she was carrying that wretched piece of cheese. She held it out to him, and he took it. Then she fainted.

The Temporary Death of Mrs. Ayres

The Temporary Death of Mrs. Ayres

Mrs. Ayres had no idea of doing it when she wakened that morning. She had eaten her usual light breakfast, reading the papers as she did so. After the war news her stomach had tied itself in its usual knot. But it had been doing that ever since Pearl Harbor. Only lately she had noticed a small tight pain where the back of her neck met her skull. Nerves, she thought.

She picked up the calendar beside her bed. It was a full day: the Red Cross in the morning, a hospital meeting and a First Aid class in the afternoon, the family to dinner that night, and — good heavens, it was the last day to pay her quarterly income tax. She lay back on her pillows and tentatively moved her feet, which hurt. She must find time to buy some low-heeled shoes. After all at her age a woman had a right to care for her feet.

She thought resentfully of the income tax. She had done her bit through two wars. In the first she had almost lost Herbert. They had been married only a week when he left, to take yellow fever in Cuba and nearly die of it. And in the last war Joe— She closed her eyes. Joe in a steel helmet going to France. Singing Tipperary along bad French roads, and at last coming back, rather quiet and sheepishly showing a box containing a bit of shrapnel which had at one time been a part of his anatomy.

Yes, she had done her bit. And now here was another war, with everything going up, except her modest dividends, and sooner or later Andy—

A hot bath relaxed her somewhat and helped her feet. She creamed her face and crawled back into bed for a minute before she dressed. With her hair loose about her face she did not look her age, and Annie the cook, coming for the day's orders, told her so.

"Like that you could pass for fifty," she said. Annie had been with her for thirty years, and sometimes Mrs. Ayres felt that the house belonged to her. "My double boiler's wearing out," she would say, or "My icebox needs the repair man." Now she stood inside the door.

"What are we eating today?" she inquired.

"Oh, Annie! Just after breakfast!"

"You have to eat," said Annie firmly. "Anyhow it's the family night."

Mrs. Ayres saw that it was hopeless. Her mind ranged wildly among the food animals and took a leap to poultry.

"We might have chicken."

"We had chicken last Thursday."

"Well, how about steak and mushrooms?"

"Mr. Joe can't eat mushrooms."

Mrs. Ayres sighed.

"All right, Annie," she said. "Steak without mushrooms and maybe a strawberry shortcake. Unless"—she added cautiously—"strawberries take too much sugar."

They did, so they compromised on a prune *soufflé*. She felt guilty as Annie disappeared. Steak was expensive. But she had clung to the weekly dinners, partly because since Herbert's death she had been lonely, and partly, she knew, because she still wanted them to look to her for the little extras of living. They were all hard up, poor children, she thought. So was she, desperately, but she had not told them. They had worries enough of their own.

Annie had carried up the mail with her breakfast, and Mrs. Ayres sat up in bed to look it over. It consisted of seven appeals for wartime charities, three others from charities she had always supported—but how could she now, with the government taking so much of her income?—two pamphlets from Washington urging her to buy War Bonds, and a rather bulky letter from her sister-in-law. The tightness at the back of her head came back when she opened it. As she had expected, it contained a number of samples.

"Dear Margaret," Isabel wrote. "I had expected to be with you by this time for my annual visit. But Marian's fiancé"—Marian was Isabel's daughter—"has leave from the Navy in ten days, so the wedding is earlier than we expected. I have the reception to attend to, so you will have to do some shopping for me in a hurry. I enclose samples, all marked. Also the size of Marian's slippers. The bridesmaids' hats are to be of tulle, colors enclosed, and—"

Mrs. Ayres looked frantically at her calendar. It offered no comfort, however, so she got out of bed and began to dress. She was still dressing when Beulah, her daughter, called her up. Her voice was urgent.

"Look, mother," she said. "David's just fallen and broken a tooth. Could you take him to the dentist's? I know it's your Red Cross morning, but Jane's been sick all night and I can't leave her."

Mrs. Ayres agreed, rather shiveringly. She hated taking children to the dentist's, and she liked going to the Red Cross. It was as though, by working for other women's sons, she had an excuse for her own. Not for Joe, of course. He was too old. But Andy. She closed her eyes when she thought of Andy.

Dressed, she went downstairs. The house lay

all about her, quiet and orderly. It was a white elephant of a house nowadays, she thought. She couldn't either rent or sell it. She didn't even know how she was going to pay the taxes on it. She could hardly buy the coal to heat it. And she had had Annie and Sarah for thirty years. They were her age now, and she could not turn them off. Where would they go? What would they do? It had been bad enough to give up her car. She had missed Mike dreadfully. She had always felt safe with him. And he had made her laugh.

"Can you get through there, Mike?"

"Sure I can, ma'am. I'll just fold up the fenders a bit."

Mike was all right. He had a job in a munitions factory. But the maids would have to stay. "Even if we have to starve together," she thought wryly.

She took a bus to Beulah's. It was crowded, and she had to stand. Her feet gave her a warning twinge or two, but she forgot them when she saw Beulah's face. It was young and very pretty, and practically desperate.

"Why on earth did you ever let me get married?" she demanded. "I'd like to run away and never come back."

"Things do happen," said Mrs. Ayres comfortingly. "It isn't easy sometimes, especially when the children are small."

"That's fine, coming from you," said Beulah. "We each have our own troubles, but you still have all of them. Mother, I'm frightened. Paul's blood pressure is up."

Mrs. Ayres forced a smile.

"I wouldn't worry about that," she said. "A good many men have it these days. Paul's young. He'll get over it. I suppose," she added tentatively, "it will at least keep him out of the army."

"He wants to go to Washington. He has the chance of some war work there. It will kill him, mother. I won't let him go. I can't."

She was on the verge of tears when she went out to get David. Mrs. Ayres sat very still. The apartment was close and not too tidy, and somewhere little Jane was whimpering in her sleep. She remembered the day Paul and Beulah were married, the bride beautiful in her white satin, and carrying white orchids. The long procession of bridesmaids, the bride's cake, the champagne— She brought herself up with a start and looked in her bag.

Yes, she had Isabel's list.

David was recalcitrant. He refused to go to the dentist's until she had promised him a soldier's uniform as a reward, and Beulah laughed hysterically.

"You see?" she said. "Even the children! I think we've all gone crazy."

It was a bad morning. Mrs. Ayres's nerves

were as unstrung as loose telegraph wires when she got David back home, proudly carrying his uniform. Little Jane was no better, and Beulah had sent for the doctor. She sat by the bed for a minute or two. How many times, she thought, she had sat by little beds like this. And even bigger ones. This business of birth and life and death—

Her feet were badly swollen when she got home. In the kitchen Annie surveyed her grimly.

"You look all in," she said, with the familiarity of years of association. "What you'd better do is to crawl into bed and let me send you a poached egg on a tray."

She agreed gladly. She would rest a while, and then do Isabel's shopping, or part of it. The hospital would have to go. However, it did not happen that way. The doorbell rang, and she heard Joe's deep voice.

"Mother in?"

"Just came in, Mr. Joe," said Sarah.

"Well, tell Annie I'll have some lunch, if she has enough. Lamb chops will do. Anything handy."

Mrs. Ayres went forward. She was always excited when she saw her eldest son. But she felt apprehensive too. For Joe to leave his tottering business in the middle of the day and come uptown was almost unheard of. And Joe quite definitely had something on his mind. She assumed the air of cheerful briskness she always showed her family.

"Where in the world brings you here?" she asked. "Don't tell me you're not having dinner with me tonight?"

Joe sat down rather heavily. He looked embarrassed.

"I'm in a bit of a jam, mother," he said. "And God! How I hate coming to you!"

"Not—Dorothy?"

"Not Dorothy. No," said Joe heavily. "She's working her head off. We've had to let the nurse go, and the children are a handful. I just wondered—" He hesitated, then took the plunge. "Could you lend me two hundred dollars until the end of the month? It's these damned taxes. They're due today. I'll pay it back, of course."

He would, she thought. He always had. She looked at him, at his tired face, his thinning hair. She would have lain down and let him trample her to death. Only now, with her own bank balance so low—

"Why, of course," she said, still brightly. "They *are* dreadful, aren't they? And what are mothers for, anyhow?"

"Thanks a lot," he said. "We're cutting every corner, and I'm expecting to get word any day from Washington to start work. I hate like hell coming to you."

"Don't be an idiot," she said. "I'm a useless

old woman. If I can't help my children what fun I would lose!"

She made out the check, which reduced her bank balance to practically nothing, and Joe ate a hearty lunch. The household had managed the chops somehow. But he was not talkative. She suspected that he hated borrowing from her, as though it somehow impugned his manhood.

"How's Andy?" she said. "I haven't heard from him for a day or two."

Andy was her baby. She could never think of him as anything else. And now Andy wanted to enlist and go into aviation. The mere mention of his name had set her hands to shaking. She hid them in her lap, so Joe would not notice them.

"He's all right, I guess."

"He hasn't quarreled with Edna?"

"Not that I know of."

But he was not communicative. Edna was more or less engaged to Andy, and just now she was going about in a uniform while Andy wasn't. She was all for the aviation thing, but then she hadn't borne him, or watched him cut his first teeth, or worried over him for years on end. And Edna had no imagination. She did not lie awake nights seeing him somewhere in the sky, that sky which once had meant God and his angels to her, and now meant only death, and Andy alone in it.

Joe was watching her, so she smiled and told

him about Isabel's letter. He swore softly.

"Why can't she come on and do it herself?" he demanded.

But she shuddered at the thought. Isabel's loud voice all over the house, her complete conviction that only her own affairs mattered, the service she demanded, the fact that the maids loathed her— She shook her head.

"I don't think I could bear that," she said. "I'll manage somehow."

He looked happier when he left. He kissed her warmly, and her heart swelled. These were the moments for which she lived, to be useful, to be needed by her children. She asked nothing more. It never occurred to her that she had drawn her circle too small or too tight.

She did some of Isabel's shopping that afternoon. It was difficult, trying to think she was Marian, or one of the bridesmaids. The hats she tried on made her look older than God, she thought, and incredibly tired. And some of the things could not be bought at all.

"It's the war, madam. So many priorities, and of course nothing from France."

Always the war, she thought, as at last she limped to a bus. Why couldn't we just go along as we were? Twelve years of depression—surely that had been enough, without all this.

She had just got home when the word came about Jane. She had slipped off her shoes and had begun to feel relaxed. Then she was called to the telephone, and it was Beulah.

"We're at the hospital," she said. "They're operating in half an hour. Appendix. You needn't come unless you want to, mother, but I knew you'd want to know."

Mrs. Ayres felt slightly dizzy. Her heart began to thump.

"Of course I'm coming," she said. "It isn't serious, you know, darling. She's a strong child."

Nevertheless, her heart thumped all the way to the hospital, although she was resolutely matter-of-fact when she went into the room where Paul and Beulah were waiting. Beulah had lighted a cigarette and Paul was at the window, staring out. The poor children, she thought, already confronting life and death. And this was a load she could not lift.

"I wouldn't worry too much," she said briskly. "It's not much more than pulling a tooth these days."

"Oh, for heaven's sake, mother," said Beulah, her voice tight. "Don't try to be cheerful. She's my baby."

"I've seen you all through it, Beulah, and you're all here."

But they did not listen. Mrs. Ayres sat down. Her heart still felt as though it were pumping lead. Paul left the window and took to pacing the floor, and Beulah smoked endlessly. Mrs.

Ayres felt rather short of breath, and then at last came the roll of rubber wheels in the hall. Little Jane had come back, and a nurse came in, smiling.

Mrs. Ayres tried to get up. It was all right, she thought. Everything was over. Then she realized that her knees would not hold her. She sat down and leaned her head against the back of the chair. She was still there when Tommy Stewart came in, in his operating clothes. He gave her a quick look and felt her pulse.

"See here," he said, "what are you doing anyhow? Trying to faint?"

She had known him for years. His father had brought her children into the world. It seemed queer that little Tommy Stewart had grown into this quiet self-confident man who dealt with life and death, and who now held her wrist in capable fingers.

"I'm perfectly all right," she said. "I've had a trying day. That's all."

"Well, I can save the mothers and fathers," he said drily. "But the grandmothers—! How long since you've been gone over?"

"I don't remember."

"I thought so. Go home and go to bed. I'll stop by about six. That all right?"

"But Jane—"

"She's fine." He was impatient. "By the day after tomorrow she won't know anything's happened to her. Why can't you let your family carry its own troubles? They're perfectly able and willing to."

She went home in a taxi, feeling guilty and extravagant. But she did not go to bed immediately. Andy was waiting for her in the lower hall. He was pacing back and forward, with his hands in his pockets and the familiar forward thrust of his head that she knew so well. She sat down on a hall chair and looked at him. He was the handsomest of her children, and the most unpredictable.

"What is it, Andy? Is anything wrong?"

"Not unless it's wrong for you, mother."

"I don't know what you mean," she said feebly.

He stood in front of her, looking down at her.

"I think you do, mother. I've held off. You've had your share of war, with father and Joe. And in a way I'm the only one you have left, with Beulah and Joe both married. But I'll have to go now. I only—well, I'd like to think you are willing. That's all."

So it had come, after all, she thought tiredly. Her hostages to fate, her contributions to charities, her Red Cross work, her bundles to Britain, even her prayers—all that, and they had won her exactly nothing.

"You mustn't put it up to me, Andy," she said, her voice tight and thin. "It isn't fair."

"I'm not putting it up to you, mother. I only want— I suppose in the old days they called it your blessing." He smiled down at her. "Maybe it will bring me luck!"

She tried to return his smile.

"Of course you have that, darling," she said. "What about Edna? Is she willing?"

"Edna's in uniform, working her head off. How do you think I like that?"

"If it's a uniform you want," she began feebly. But he threw his head up. It frightened her. "I'm sorry," she said. "Don't think of me, darling. Don't even think of Edna. It's your life that's at stake."

"It's my country that's at stake," he said grimly.

She was in bed when Tommy Stewart came. She was thinking that after all it might be rather peaceful just to die. Not to worry any more, not to think about war, or operations, or even income taxes. When Tommy came in she was lying still in her bed, her hands folded across her breast and her eyes closed.

"What on earth is that for?" he said suspiciously.

"I was wondering what would happen if I were to die," she said, not opening her eyes. "You haven't a lily to put in my hand, have you?"

Tommy laughed.

"No lily," he said. "And you'd probably be

surprised about what would happen."

She opened her eyes.

"What?"

"Nothing much. Things would go along all right. You're just feeding your vanity, you know. Now let's get that blood pressure. What do you bet it's low?"

She eyed him resentfully. What did he know about her life and its problems? Or the sort of day she had had? She did not speak while he put the tubing around her arm and blew it up. When it was over he grinned at her.

"Low is right," he said. "Take it easy for a while. Let the family get along. It might even like it. And stay in bed if you can for a couple of weeks. Jane's all right. Don't worry about her. Don't worry about anything."

He went away, whistling cheerfully. She was still indignant. Feeding her vanity, she thought bitterly! So that was the way the young felt about the old. This was their world. It wasn't the old who made wars. It was the young who wanted to fight, to get out of the rut, to find adventure, to have someone else do their thinking for them. Even Joe—she knew Joe wanted to go. He couldn't, of course, but there it was. As to the rest of it—

But she was very tired. Her feet began to feel better, and after a while she dozed. She was still asleep when Sarah brought her the telegram. It was from Isabel, and it was a typical Isabel message.

"Think best to do shopping personally. Arrive with Marian four-thirty tomorrow. Staying only four or five days. Please have car meet us."

She lay staring at it. Isabel at any time was a trial. Isabel and Marian together at any time was a catastrophe. She groaned and sitting up in bed looked at Sarah.

"It's from Mrs. Warwick," she said weakly. "She's coming tomorrow. She and Miss Marian. She doesn't even know I've laid up the car."

Sarah's face tightened.

"You can't have them. The doctor said you were to rest."

Mrs. Ayres looked at the clock.

"It's too late to stop them, Sarah. They've taken the evening train. I'll have to have them."

"You wouldn't if you were dead."

"Good gracious, Sarah!"

But Sarah did not smile.

"A body can work herself to death for people," she said darkly. "And when they're gone, what? Annie says it's like taking a thumb out of a bowl of soup."

"Well, I'm not dead," said Mrs. Ayres sharply. "You'll have to fix two rooms for them. They don't like being together."

Sarah sniffed and went out, and Mrs. Ayres got out of bed stiffly and prepared to dress for

190

dinner. She always dressed for these family re-
unions. It pleased her to sit at the head of her
table, looking attractive and as young as possible; to have the boys say she didn't look her age,
and Beulah speak about her hair. But her high-
heeled slippers hurt damnably, and with the
thought of slippers she remembered. All those
packages on their way West, and Isabel and
Marian coming on to buy them after all!

Suddenly she knew she could not face Isabel.
And not Isabel only. She wanted to escape from
life for a time; to lie back and rest, even to
forget the war and the price she might soon have
to pay for it.

She looked over at Herbert's picture, slightly
faded in its frame. Herbert had had very definite
ideas about things.

"I'm so dreadfully tired, Bert," she said apologetically. "And everything's so frightful."

But of course Herbert said nothing. He merely
continued to look firm.

The dinner was gay that night. It was, she
thought, as though having lived through today,
they were leaving tomorrow to take care of itself.
Perhaps that was because they were still young.
Perhaps one was only old when tomorrow became important. It wasn't true, she considered,
that age lived in the past. Who wanted to live on
memories? Age looked ahead. It had to.

Nevertheless she watched them proudly. Joe

and his Dorothy, her hands reddened with unaccustomed housework but her smile serene; Paul and Beulah, relaxed before going back to the hospital, even Andy, a trifle wary but with his jaw set, and only eyes for Edna.

And it was Edna, in a way, who spilled the beans. She was a small, determined young woman, still in uniform that night and with a horrifying habit of speaking her mind. So in a brief pause she did exactly that.

"I do hope, Mother Ayres," she said, "that you are going to be a sport and let go of Andy."

There was an appalled silence. Mrs. Ayres felt herself stiffening.

"Let go of Andy?" she said. "I don't know what you mean."

"Well, let him go, anyhow. It's the same thing, isn't it? Send him off with a smile." She looked around the table, rather startled. "Sorry," she said. "I'm not noted for my tact. But after all—"

She subsided then. Joe's face was furious and Andy had flushed. Mrs. Ayres rallied herself.

"I can't live my children's lives, Edna," she said.

But Edna too had rallied.

"I think," she said clearly, "that a good many mothers do that without knowing it. Take these family dinners! They're fine. They're grand. I love to come. But just the same—"

"Oh, for God's sake shut up, Edna," Andy

said wearily. "I can manage my own life, and mother knows it."

Things went on smoothly enough after that, although there was tension all around the table. But Mrs. Ayres had an uncomfortable feeling that she was a sort of bone and that the family was quarreling over her. That mustn't happen, she thought wildly. She must get away somewhere, die a little death, bury herself beyond finding. Like a bone. Like a thumb out of a—

At the end of the meal she rapped on her glass and smiled at them all.

"I have a little something to say," she told them. "It's not really important. But Tommy Stewart took my blood pressure today. It's rather low."

She could see them, their concerned faces turned toward her, the sudden silence.

"He thinks I need a rest cure. A—well, a really absolute rest cure. It sounds silly, doesn't it?"

"What does he mean, an absolute rest cure?" Joe said. "Of course you need a rest. We've all known it for months."

She smiled again, reassuringly.

"It's to be rather drastic," she said. "The idea is to cut myself off entire. I'll not be seeing even any of you. No radio, no telephone, no newspapers, no visitors. I'm not even going to talk to Sarah and Annie. It's to be—well, exactly as

193

though one took a thumb out of a bowl of soup."

They looked astounded.

"A bowl of soup?" said Beulah. "Mother, what on earth do you mean?"

Mrs. Ayres flushed faintly.

"I'm sorry," she said. "I really hadn't meant to say that. It's just that Sarah—but never mind. I thought I'd start tonight. You could all see me settled and then forget me. For two weeks only, of course. I couldn't stand it any longer."

It was Paul who broke the incredulous silence, Paul with his pleasant eyes and his soft voice.

"Does it have to be so drastic?" he asked. "No flowers, no baby pillows, no pretty bed-jackets?"

She felt grateful to him.

"None," she said lightly. "Also no taxes to think about, no Isabel to worry about, and no tight slippers. I think I really want to rest my feet."

They could understand that. It relieved them. They cheered enormously, and things began to move fast. Sarah and Annie were brought in, looking dazed when the matter was explained to them. The radio was carried out of her bedroom, the telephone shut off. They made a game of it, and at last they formed a procession and escorted her upstairs, singing Hail, Hail, The Gang's All Here. It was all very cheerio, and Mrs. Ayres had all she could do to keep from

194

howling like a wolf, especially when Joe, big dependable Joe, lingered behind the others. He stood in the doorway and looked at her gravely.

"Pretty weary, aren't you, mother?" he said. "Glad to get rid of us for a bit."

She denied it.

"It's not that. It's never that, Joe."

"Then what is it?"

She tried to think. She wasn't even sure herself.

"I'll have to find my way around somehow," she told him. "This is a new world, Joe. I haven't accepted it yet. But I must. Only don't ask me to like it. I can't."

When he had gone she sat down and took off her slippers. She wondered if after all her grand talk about a new world it wasn't her feet anyhow. But after the front door had closed and quiet settled down over the house she felt suddenly frightened. She had cut herself off from them deliberately, and things moved so terrifyingly fast these days. Her hands were cold as she started to undress.

She was almost ready for bed when she remembered the income tax check, still unsigned. She sighed, put on her clothes again and went downstairs. The house looked lived in, she thought, after the family had been there. The girls' cigarettes, stained with lipstick, the ashes from Andy's pipe, the stub of Joe's cigar, the crushed cushions, the chairs moved about. Usually she straightened it, but that night she did not touch it. It was as though, by leaving it as it was, they were still with her. She signed her check and went out to the mailbox at the corner with the envelope. It was a bright moonlit night, and a man with an air warden's brassard on his left arm was standing on the corner.

Suddenly she felt the need of someone to talk to.

"Any chance of a raid?" she inquired.

"It's a good night for them," he said genially. "But I guess they're pretty busy on the other side."

He smiled down at her small rather fragile figure.

"We'll beat them yet," he said. "Just wait and see."

"I hope so," she said politely.

When she went back she closed the street door behind her with a strange feeling of finality. The last thing she did was to carry up an armload of books she had never had time to read, and she closed her bedroom door rather slowly, as though she were reluctant to close it at all.

Nevertheless she slept that night as she had not slept for years. The telephone, which usually started early, did not ring at all, and if Sarah grinned cheerfully when she brought the breakfast tray, she did not speak. While Mrs. Ayres took her bath she changed and cleaned the room. After that she disappeared.

Thus began the two weeks of Mrs. Ayres' temporary death.

On her lunch tray that day there was a prescription blank from Tommy Stewart, and written on it were just three words: "Good for you." They were the last communication she held with the active everyday world for some time. Or almost the last, although Isabel's eruption was a one-sided affair.

It was late in the afternoon when the taxi drove up to the door. Mrs. Ayres could hear a number of bags being taken out, followed by the ringing of the doorbell. Rather guiltily she crawled out of bed and listened.

"Well, Sarah, how are you?" said Isabel's high voice. "Do you mind bringing in the bags? Marian, a quarter tip's too much for that taxi."

"I'm sorry," said Sarah, courteously but inexorably. "No visitors are allowed, Mrs. Warwick."

"What do you mean, no visitors? I wired her I was coming."

"Yes'm, but she isn't seeing anybody. She says she's dead."

Even up in her room Mrs. Ayres heard Isabel snort.

"What sort of nonsense is that?" she demanded indignantly. "She *says* she's dead!"

"That's what she says, Ma'am. No visitors, no

family, no papers, no radio, no telephone, no—"

"She must have lost her mind," Isabel said in a loud voice. "I'm going to see her. Get out of my way, Sarah."

Mrs. Ayres hastily retreated and locked her door. She was just in time. The attack on the door was short but noisy, but even Isabel, however, was daunted at last by the complete silence. With a final statement that Mrs. Ayres should be committed to a lunatic asylum she finally departed. There was the sound of innumerable bags being thrown into a taxi, Marian's high protest, and then once more peace. Oh wonderful beautiful peace.

By the third day Mrs. Ayres' feet felt much better. They even looked better. The rule of silence still obtained. Sarah brought her tray and took it away. Once or twice she looked about to burst into speech, but Mrs. Ayres merely shook her head. She was eating better, and her bathroom scale showed she had gained a pound. Once or twice she glanced at her knitting—for the Red Cross—but she did not touch it. For she knew by that time that what she was really escaping was the war.

Mostly she read and slept. But by the fourth day she began again to worry about the family. They could get into such dreadful messes. There was the time before her marriage when Beulah had threatened to go to Hollywood. A new mink coat had stopped her, but of course there were no new mink coats nowadays. And the time Joe's Dorothy had come to her crying and said she was going to have another baby, and she didn't want it. And of course Andy had fallen in love with a married woman while he was in college and had threatened to kill himself unless he got her. A trip around the world had cured him, and Herbert had had a fit and almost apoplexy. But there it was.

The poor children, she thought, and wondered what they were doing without her.

By the end of the week she was beginning to be restless. One day she got out her old letters, Herbert's first letter after their marriage when he was on his way to Cuba and the Spanish War. "My darling wife: How wonderful that I may call you that! I still can't believe my luck" — only he had written it beleive. He never could spell — "and that you are really my own girl now. It is only an hour since I kissed you good-bye and we started South. The fellows are singing and yelling all around me on this train. You would think it was a picnic! But I don't feel like singing. All I can think about is you."

There was quite a bit more of it. It differed somewhat from the last one he had written her before he took sick and left her for good. That one merely said, "Dear Margaret," and went on rather peevishly to state that she had forgotten to pack his dress studs, and for God's sake to send them to him by airmail.

She had loved him dearly. She had not even resented the change from lover to middle-aged husband. But he had been gone for many years, and sometimes she wondered, in case she were to see him again in another world, just whether she would know him. It would be so frightfully embarrassing if she didn't.

Her hands shook a little as she took up the thin bundle of letters from Joe in France in the last war. They all began "Dearest Mother," and she tried to feel again some of the heroic endurance with which she had sent him away. But she did not. Perhaps war hadn't been such a dirty business then. Soldiers had fought soldiers, not tried to kill the plain people, not rained death from the sky on children. But she found it hard to remember that war; only Joe coming home, rather quiet, and showing her rather sheepishly his little box.

"The nurse said you might want to see it, mother."

Well, now it was all to be done over again, and here she lay in her bed, pretending that it was not. It wasn't any good, she thought drearily. She couldn't shut out the sound of newsboys crying extras, or the sound of planes at night shooting like bullets across the sky. Whether she liked it or not the war was here. It was, so to speak, on her doorstep, and closing the door did not shut it out.

By the beginning of the second week only sheer stubbornness kept her in her room. She had been an idiot, she reflected. Her feet felt better, but her mind was running in frantic circles. She lost the pound she had gained, and her trays went down almost untouched. In the kitchen Annie gazed at them and banged the dishes.

"Worrying about *them*," she said.

"Well, I'm not going to be the one to tell her," said Sarah.

But it was not the family by that time. Not entirely, at least. Shut up comfortably in her quiet room Mrs. Ayres was fighting a small battle of her own. It began with her going back over her own life. It had been, she thought, a very American one; her free, easy childhood, her marriage, the births of her children, the years with Herbert. Curiously, Herbert began to loom very large in this new picture. Not Herbert, dying in the very bed in which she lay, and saying: "You've been a damned good wife to me, Margaret." But the Herbert of the last war.

He had never been quite the same after it. He had taken Joe's going to France too hard. Nevertheless he had wanted him to go.

"Got to let the children grow up," he had said. "And we can't let those devils get away with murder. If I wasn't too old I'd go myself. Got to stop the thing somehow."

And during that second week she began to see Herbert more and more clearly. He had been very quiet while Joe was overseas. He had even made an attempt later on to get over himself. That was when he found he wasn't as well a man as he had thought he was. Not that he made a fuss about it.

"Liver or kidneys or something," he had told her. "Nothing to worry about. Only there's a job to be done, or those God-damned Huns will be over here, goose-stepping on our necks. And I can't do it."

What would he have thought now? In his inarticulate way he had been deeply American. He had knocked a man's hat off one day when he didn't remove it as the flag passed in a parade. The man had fought back, and they had both been arrested. Even now she smiled when she remembered his furious homecoming that night.

"Where on earth have you been, Bert?"

"I've been in jail. Where the hell do you think I've been?"

She even found herself, during those last days of her temporary death, defending herself to him.

"It's such a dreadful war, Bert," she would say. "We thought the last one was bad, but this is different. And I'm not young any more. I get

202

tired so easily, and I can't stand shocks."

But other women all over the world were standing shocks. Shocks and horror. While she lay there in her bed death was abroad everywhere. And she could almost hear Herbert's answer. He had said it about Joe.

"We can't let other people's sons fight this for us, my girl. It's our job, too."

She got up one night and held his picture to the light, but there was no relenting in it. It was as if it asked her what she herself was doing, shut up in her room with a world afire.

The last night of her temporary death was hot. She could not sleep, although the city was very still. She could never remember it so still. It was as though a great hand had settled over it and smothered it. As though indeed it had died, and she alone remained alive. At midnight she got up in the dark, put on a dressing gown and slippers and went down the stairs. She felt her way to the front door and opened it, to find herself still in darkness. There were no street lights. No cars moved. Even the houses across the street were black shadows, and she drew in her breath sharply.

A figure moved beside her.

"Who's that?" said a familiar voice.

"Oh, Mike!" she said. "Mike, what is it?"

She could not see him. He was only a sturdy, reassuring voice out of the dark.

"Nothing to worry about," he said. "Heard there was an 'alert' about a quarter of an hour ago. I thought I'd come over. That roof of yours ain't too good."

"You mean they're coming?"

"Well, maybe they are, maybe not," said Mile. "I got a bucket of sand here, just in case they drop some of these here fire bombs. You feeling better?"

"I'm feeling like a wicked woman, Mike. I've been running away."

"I guess we all want to do that sometimes," said Mike comfortably.

She sat down on the doorstep. All those children, she thought, asleep in the city, all the tired men and women, and if not tonight perhaps some other night death might fly over them and then drop on them. From far overhead came the droning of planes, but Mike was calm. He cocked an ear at the sky.

"Reckon they're our fellows," he said. "They sure keep a watch. No trouble while they're around."

This was what Andy wanted to do, she thought; to see that all over the world tired children, and men and women too, had the right to sleep; to live and work and sleep in safety and freedom.

"I've been blind and selfish," she said to herself. "I've held him back. I've tried to hold them all. Herbert was right. I've played God long enough. Now it's in His hands. I suppose it always was."

All at once the city lights began to come on. She stood up and looked at them. Never before had light seemed so beautiful. So rare and beautiful. She drew a long breath. Beside her Mike was grinning. He had picked up his bucket.

"Well, I guess that's that," he said. "Wouldn't want this sand to build castles with, would you?"

"I've been building castles on sand all my life, Mike. That's over."

She watched him down the street, his sturdy shoulders, his heavy muscular body. He had fought in the last war. He might still fight in this. But he had done the thing that came to hand. He had brought sand for her roof and stood by for trouble. There must be things that even she could do. . . .

She gave what Joe called her Lazarus dinner the next night. Up to the last minute she kept her rule of silence, and when she started down the staircase they were waiting in the hall below, their faces turned up to her. What a handsome lot they were, she thought. It was like a miracle. They were holding flowers and little parcels, and her heart swelled with pride.

"How are you, mother?"

"I feel wonderful."

That was when she saw Andy's uniform. She clutched dizzily at the stair-rail. This was the test, she knew. The last two weeks had been really a preparation for it. She steadied her voice.

"So I have another soldier son," she said. "I'm very proud, Andy."

They crowded around her then. They had missed her frightfully, they said. And they had news of all sorts. Paul had got his job in Washington and his blood pressure was down. Joe's contract had come through. The grandchildren were well. And when she had a chance Edna—without her uniform and looking pretty and rather chastened—made her a handsome apology.

"I suppose," she ended, "I hadn't realized what an anchor you are."

Mrs. Ayres met it gallantly.

"Only an anchor shouldn't try to run a ship," she said.

But the sense of strangeness persisted through the dinner. They were excited and noisy. They had work, plans, even hopes. Apparently the future did not worry them. They shrieked with laughter when Sarah produced a hideous sugar shaker which allowed them only a spoonful at a time. Beulah was learning to ride a bicycle, so she could get around Washington streets, and she found Joe's check for what he had borrowed from her under her napkin.

Yes, it was their world, she thought. They loved her, but they did not need her. They hadn't really needed her for years. She felt rather empty as she smiled at them.

Andy held her for a moment before they left. "It's all right, mother, isn't it?"

"Of course, darling."

There were no cars at the door when she saw them out, but they did not seem to mind. She stood watching as long as she could see them: Andy's uniform under the street lights, Joe's big solid shoulders, Beulah's bright hair. Then they were out of sight, and she made a queer little gesture of renunciation. As though they were gone—as indeed they were.

The city was quiet. Overhead a plane droned, keeping its watch over the sleeping town. When at last she went inside she felt that one phase of her life was over and another one beginning. But she was not sleepy. Upstairs in her room she stood for a minute in front of Herbert's picture, and it seemed to her that it looked gentler, and not at all that of the Herbert who had been peevish about his dress studs and for God's sake to send them at once by airmail.

"They've gone, Bert," she said. "It's all right, even about Andy. Only what am I to do? There must be something."

She put out the light, but she did not sleep.

She felt strong and rested, as she had not felt for years, and at last she got up and dressed. When she reached the front door again the street was empty. It was hard to believe that bloody war was all over the earth, and that she was finally and at last alone. She felt like a ghost, making signs that nobody answered.

She was still there when the air warden came along. She hailed him with a sort of desperation.

"Can you stop a minute?" she asked.

"Certainly. Need any help?"

"No," she said, rather breathlessly. "I just wondered—I thought maybe I could do something. You see," she added, "in a way I've been dead for two weeks, and I can't sleep. There must be something."

He eyed her. She did not look crazy. She looked small and sane and somehow appealing. He took off his helmet, which was painted white so it could be seen in a blackout, and rubbed his hand over his hair.

"You mean tonight?" he asked incredulously.

"Right now. This minute. If I could even walk with you it would help."

He was puzzled. He had seen hysteria of all kinds, the terror that walks at night in war. But she did not seem hysterical. She seemed merely lonely.

"I don't know," he said. "There's a girl on duty at the air raid post around the corner. Telephone, you know. She's worked in a factory all day, and her relief hasn't come. You might sit there while she gets a bit of sleep. Or isn't that what you mean?"

"It sounds wonderful," said Mrs. Ayres.

She felt happier than she had felt for a long time as she waited for him to make the arrangements. It wasn't much, she thought. But after all wasn't that what this war was about? That weary people, men and women and children, could sleep in peace; could live and work and sleep.

Above her the sky was filled with stars. Some day Andy would be up there. But perhaps Herbert was there too, and maybe God and all his angels.

She waited serenely, while she put her family and the beaten weary world into their hands.

The Butler's Christmas Eve

The Butler's Christmas Eve

William stood in the rain waiting for the bus. In the fading daylight he looked rather like a freshly washed eighty-year-old and beardless Santa Claus, and underneath his raincoat he clutched a parcel which contained a much-worn nightshirt, an extra pair of socks, a fresh shirt and a brand-new celluloid collar. It also contained a pint flask of the best Scotch whisky.

Not that William drank, or at least not to speak of. The whisky was a gift, and in more than one way it was definitely contraband. It was whisky which had caused his trouble.

The Christmas Eve crowd around him was wet but amiable.

"Look, mama, what have you done with the suitcase?"

"What do you think you're sitting on? A bird cage?"

The crowd laughed. The rain poured down. The excited children were restless. They darted about, were lost and found again. Women scolded.

"You stand right here, Johnny. Keep under this umbrella. That's your new suit."

When the bus came along one of them knocked William's package into the gutter, and he found himself shaking with anxiety. But the bottle was all right. He could feel it, still intact. The Old Man would have it, all right, Miss Sally or no Miss Sally; the Old Man, left sitting in a wheelchair with one side of his big body dead and nothing warm in his stomach to comfort him. Just a year ago tonight on Christmas Eve William had slipped him a small drink to help him sleep, and Miss Sally had caught him at it.

She had not said anything. She had kissed her grandfather good-night and walked out of the room. But the next morning she had come into the pantry where William was fixing the Old Man's breakfast tray and dismissed him, after fifty years.

"I'm sorry, William. But you know he is forbidden liquor."

William put down the Old Man's heated egg cup and looked at her.

"It was only because it was Christmas Eve, Miss Sally. He was kind of low, with Mr. Tony gone and everything."

She went white at that, but her voice was even.

"I am trying to be fair," she said. "But even without this— You have worked a long time, and grandfather is too heavy for you to handle. I need a younger man, now that—"

She did not finish. She did not say that her young husband had enlisted in the Navy after Pearl Harbor, and that she had fought tooth and nail against it. Or that she suspected both her grandfather and William of supporting him.

William gazed at her incredulously.

"I've handled him, one way and another, for fifty years, Miss Sally."

"I know all that. But I've talked to the doctor. He agrees with me."

He stood very still. She couldn't do this to him, this girl he had raised, and her father before her. She couldn't send him out at his age to make a life for himself, after living a vicarious one in this house for half a century. But he saw helplessly that she could and that she meant to.

"When am I to go?" he asked.

"It would be kinder not to see him again, wouldn't it?"

"You can't manage alone, Miss Sally," he said stubbornly. But she merely made a little gesture with her hands.

"I'm sorry, William. I've already arranged for someone else."

He took the breakfast tray to the Old Man's door and gave it to the nurse. Then he went upstairs to his room and standing inside looked around him. This had been his room for most of his life. On the dresser was the faded snapshot of the Old Man as a Major in the Rough Riders during the Spanish War. There was a picture of Miss Sally's father, his only son, who had not come home from France in 1918. There was a very new one of Mr. Tony, young and good-looking and slightly defiant, taken in his new Navy uniform. And of course there were pictures of Miss Sally herself, ranging from her baby days to the one of her, smiling and lovely, in her wedding dress.

William had helped to rear her. Standing there he remembered the day when she was born. The Major—he was Major Bennett then, not the Old Man—had sent for him when he heard the baby's mother was dead.

"Well," he said heavily, "it looks as though we've got a child to raise. A girl at that! Think we can do it?"

"We've done harder things, sir," said William.

"All right," said the Major. "But get this, William, I want no spoiled brat around the place. If I find you spoiling her, by the Lord Harry I'll fire you."

"I won't spoil her," William had said sturdily. "But she'll probably be as stubborn as a mule."

"Now why the hell do you say that?" the Major had roared.

216

But William had only smiled.

So she had grown up. She was lovable, but she was wild as a March wind and as stubborn as the Bennetts had always been. Then — it seemed almost no time to William — she met Mr. Tony, and one day she was walking down a church aisle on her grandfather's arm, looking beautiful and sedate, and when she walked out again she was a married woman.

The old house had been gay after that. It was filled with youth and laughter. Then one day Miss Sally had gone to the hospital to have her baby, and her grandfather, gray of face, had waited for the news. William had tried to comfort him.

"I understand it's a perfectly normal process, sir," he said. "They are born every day. Millions of them."

"Get your smug face out of here," roared the Major. "You and your millions! What the hell do I care about them? It's my girl who's in trouble."

He was all right then. He was even all right when the message came that it was over, and Miss Sally and Mr. Tony had a ten-minute-old son. But going out of the hospital he had staggered and fallen, and he had never walked again. That was when the household began to call him the Old Man. Behind his back, of course.

It was tragic, because Miss Sally had had no

trouble at all. She wakened at the hospital to learn that she had borne a man-child, asked if he had the proper number of fingers and toes, stated flatly that she had no intention of raising him for purposes of war, and then asked for a cigarette.

That had been two years ago, and she had come home on Christmas Eve. Mr. Tony had a little tree for the baby in the Old Man's bedroom, with Miss Sally's battered wax angel on the top, and the Old Man lay in his bed and looked at it.

"I suppose this kind of thing will save us, in the end," he said to William. "Damn it, man, people will go on having babies, and the babies will have Christmas trees, long after Hitler is dead and rotted."

The baby of course had not noticed the tree, and there was nothing to indicate that a year later William would be about to be dismissed, or that Mr. Tony, feverishly shaking a rattle before his sleeping offspring, would be in his country's uniform and somewhere on the high seas.

It was a bad year, in a way. It had told on Miss Sally, William thought. Her grandfather had taken his stroke badly. He would lie for hours, willing that stubborn will of his to move an arm, a leg, even a finger, on the stricken side. Nothing happened, of course, and at last he had accepted it, wheelchair and all. William had helped to care for him, turning his big body when the nurse changed the sheets, bathing him, when he roared that he would be eternally damned if he would allow any woman to wash him. And during the long hours of the night it had been William who sat with him while he could not sleep.

Yet Miss Sally had taken it bravely.

"He cared for me all my life," she said. "Now I can care for him. William and I."

She had done it, too. William had to grant her that. She had turned a wing of the ground floor over to him, with a porch where he could sit and look out at the sea. She gave him time and devotion. Until Pearl Harbor, that is, and the night when Mr. Tony had slipped into the Old Man's room while William was playing chess with him, and put his problem up to them.

"You know, Sally," he said. "I can't even talk to her about this war. But she's safe here, and the boy too. And—well, somebody's got to fight."

The Old Man had looked down at that swollen helpless hand of his, lying in his lap.

"I see," he said. "You want to go, of course?"

"It isn't a question of wanting, is it?"

"It is, damn it," said the Old Man fiercely. "I wanted to go to Cuba. Her father couldn't get to France fast enough. I wouldn't give a tinker's curse for the fellow who doesn't want to go.

But"—his voice softened—"it will hurt Sally like hell, son. She's had enough of war."

It had hurt her. She had fought it tooth and nail. But Tony had enlisted in the Navy almost at once, and he had gone a few days before Christmas. She did not cry when she saw him off, but she had the bleak look in her face which had never since entirely left it.

"I hope you enjoy it," she said.

"I don't expect to enjoy it, darling."

She was smiling, a strange stiff smile.

"Then why are you going?" she asked. "There are plenty of men who don't have to leave a wife to look after a baby and a helpless old man. Two old men," she said, and looked at William, standing by with the bags.

She was still not crying when after he had gone she had walked to the Old Man's room. William was there She stood in the doorway looking at them.

"I hope you're both satisfied," she said, her voice frozen. "You can sit here, safe and sound, and beat the drums all you like. But I warn you, don't beat them where I can hear them. I won't have it."

Her grandfather eyed her.

"I raised you," he said. "William and I raised you. I guess we went wrong somewhere. You're spoiled after all. And I'll beat the drums all I damn please. So will William."

Only William knew that she had not gone to bed at all that night. Some time toward morning he had seen her down on the beach in the cold, staring out at the sea.

He had trimmed the boy's tree for him that Christmas Eve. And when it was finished, with the same ancient wax angel on the top, the Old Man had suddenly asked for a drink.

"To hell with the doctors," he said. "I'll drink to Tony if it's the last thing I ever do."

As it happened, it was practically the last thing William had to do for him. For of course he had just got the liquor down when Miss Sally walked in.

She dismissed William the next morning. He had gone upstairs and packed, leaving his livery but taking the photographs with him in his battered old suitcase. When he came down the stairs Miss Sally was waiting for him. He thought she had been crying, but the bleak look was in her face again.

"I'm sorry it has to be like this, William," she said stiffly. "I have your check here, and of course if you ever need any help—"

"I've saved my money," he told her stiffly. "I can manage. If it's all right I'd like to see the baby before I go."

She nodded, and he left her and went outside. The baby toddled to him, and William picked him up and held him close.

"You be a good boy," he said. "Be a good boy and eat your cereal every day."

"Dood boy," said the child.

William stood for a minute, looking out at the winter ocean where perhaps even now Mr. Tony might be. Then he put the child down.

"Look after him, Miss Jones," he told the nurse huskily. "He's about all his great-grandfather has left."

He found he was shaking when he got into the station wagon. Paul, the chauffeur, had to lift his suitcase. Evidently he knew. He looked concerned.

"This'll be hard as hell on the Old Man," he said. "What happened, anyhow?"

"Miss Sally's upset," said William evenly. "Mr. Tony going, and all that. She has no reason to like war."

"Who does?" said Paul glumly. "What do you bet they'll get me next?"

As they left a taxi was turning in at the gate. There was a tall swarthy man inside, and William disliked him instantly. Paul grunted.

"If thats' the new fellow the Old Man will have him on his backside in a week," he said.

But so far as William knew the man was still there, and now he himself was on his way back, after a year, on some mysterious business he did not understand.

The bus rattled and roared along. The crowd

was still amiable. It called Merry Christmas to each other, and strangers talked across the aisle. It was as though for this one night in the year one common bond united them. William, clutching his parcel, felt some of its warmth infecting him.

He had been very lonely. He had taken a room in the city, but most of the people he knew had died or moved away. He took out a card to the public library, and read a good bit. And when the weather was good he sat in the park at the edge of the river, watching the ships on their way up to the Sound to join their convoys. They traveled one after the other, great grayish black monsters, like elephants in a circus holding each other's tails. Sometimes they were battleships, sometimes freighters, laden to their Plimsoll marks, their decks covered with tanks and huge crates. So close were they that once on the bridge of a destroyer he thought he saw Mr. Tony. He stood up and waved his old hat, and the young officer saluted. But it was not Tony.

When the sinkings began he watched the newspapers, his heart beating fast. Then one day he saw Tony's picture. His ship had helped to rescue a crew at sea, and Tony was smiling. He looked tired and older, however. William had cut it out and sent it to the Old Man. But the only acknowledgement had been a post card. It had been duly censored for the United States Mail, and so all it said was: "Come back, you blankety blank fool."

However, if the Old Man had his pride, so did William. He had not gone back.

Then, just a week before, he had received a telegram. It too had evidently been censored, this time for the benefit of the telegraph company. So it read: DRAT YOUR STIFF-NECKED PRIDE. COME AND SEE ME. LETTER FOLLOWS.

As the bus rattled along he got out the letter. The crowd had settled down by that time. One by one the tired children had dropped off to sleep, and even the adults looked weary, as though having worked themselves into a fine pitch of excitement they had now relapsed into patient waiting. He got out his spectacles and re-read the letter.

It was a very odd sort of letter, written as it was in the Old Man's cramped hand. It was almost as though he had expected someone else to read it. If there was anything wrong it did not say so. In fact, it alluded only to a Christmas surprise for the baby. Nevertheless the directions were puzzling. William was to arrive quietly and after dark. He was to leave his taxi at the gate, walk in, and rap on the Old Man's bedroom window. It added that the writer would get rid of the nurse if he had to drown her in the bathtub, and it closed with what sounded like an appeal. "Don't be a damn fool. I need you."

He was still thinking about it when the bus reached its destination. The rain had continued, and the crowd got out to an opening of umbrellas and another search for missing parcels. William was stiff from the long ride, and the town surprised him. It was almost completely blacked out and his taxi, when he found one, had some sort of black material over all but a narrow strip on its headlights.

"Good thing too," said the driver companionably. "We're right on the coast. Too many ships getting sunk these days. One sunk off here only a week ago. If you ask me them Germans has fellows at work right in this place. Where'd you say to go?"

"The Bennett place. Out on the beach."

The driver grinned.

"Used to drive the Major now and then," he said. "Kind of a violent talker, ain't he?"

"He's had quite a bit of trouble," said William.

"Well, his granddaughter's a fine girl," said the driver. "Know where she is tonight? Trimming a tree out at the camp. I seen her there myself."

"She always was a fine girl," said William sturdily.

The driver protested when he got out at the gate.

"Better let me take you in. It's raining cats and dogs."

225

But William shook his head.

"I want to surprise them. I know the way."

The cab drove off to an exchange of Christmas greetings, and William started for the house. There were no lights showing as he trudged along the driveway, but he could hear ahead of him the steady boom of the waves as the Atlantic rolled in, the soft hiss of the water as it rolled up the beach. Just so for fifty years had heard it. Only now it meant something new and different. It meant danger, men in ships watching against death; Mr. Tony perhaps somewhere out there in the dark, and the Old Man knowing it and listening, as he was listening.

He was relieved when he saw the garage doors open and no cars inside. He made his way cautiously around the house to the Old Man's wing, and stood listening under the bedroom window. There was no sound inside, however, and he wondered what to do. If he was asleep— Suddenly he sneezed, and he almost jumped out of his skin when a familiar voice spoke, almost at his ear.

"Come in, damn it," said the voice irritably. "What the hell are you waiting for? Want to catch your death of pneumonia?"

Suddenly William felt warm and comfortable again. This was what he had needed, to be sworn at and shouted at, to see the Old Man again, to hear him roar, or to be near him in

226

contented silence. He crawled through the window, smiling happily.

"Nothing's wrong with your voice, anyhow," he said. "Well, here I am, sir."

"And about time," said the Old Man. "Turn up the light and let me look at you. Shut the window and draw those curtains. Hah! You're flabby!"

"I've gained a little weight," William admitted.

"A little! Got a tummy like a bowl of jelly."

These amenities over they grinned at each other, and the Old Man held out his good hand.

"God," he said, "I'm glad to see you. We're going straight to the devil here. Well, a Merry Christmas to you anyhow."

"The same to you, sir."

The shook hands, and William surveyed the Old Man, sitting bolt upright in his wheelchair. He looked as truculent as ever, but some of the life had gone out of his face.

"So you ran out on me!" he said. "Why the devil didn't you turn Sally over your knee and spank her? I've seen you do it."

"I'm not as strong as I used to be," said William apologetically. The Old Man chuckled.

"She's a Bennett," he said. "Always was, always will be. But she's learning. Maybe it's the hard way, but she's learning." He eyed William. "Take off that coat, man," he said. "You're dripping all over the place. What's the package?

Anything in it but your nightshirt?"

"I've got a pint of Scotch," William admitted.

"Then what are we waiting for?" shouted the Old Man. "Sally's out. The nurse is out. Jarvis is out—that's the butler, if he is a butler and if that's his name. And the rest have gone to bed. Let's have it. It's Christmas Eve, man!"

"They oughtn't to leave you like that," William said reprovingly.

"Each of them thinks somebody else is looking after me." The Old Man chuckled. "Get some glasses. I guess you know your way. And take a look around when you get there."

William went back to the familiar rear of the house. His feet were wet and a small trickle of water had escaped his celluloid collar and gone down his back; but he walked almost jauntily. Until he saw his pantry, that is.

He did not like what he saw. The place even smelled unclean, and the silver was only half polished, the glasses he held to the light were smeared, and the floor felt sticky under his feet.

Resentfully he washed two glasses, dried them on a not too clean dish towel, and went back. The Old Man watched him from under his heavy eyebrows.

"Well, what do you think of it?" he inquired. "Is the fellow a butler?"

"He's not a good one, sir."

But the Old Man said nothing more. He took

his glass and waited until William had poured his own drink. Then he lifted the glass.

"To Tony," he said. "A safe Christmas to him, and to all the other men with the guts to fight this war."

It was like a prayer. It probably was a prayer, and William echoed it.

"To Mr. Tony," he said, "and all the rest."

Then at last the Old Man explained his letter. He didn't trust the man Jarvis. Never had. Too smooth. Sally, of course, did not suspect him, although he was damned inefficient. Anyhow what could she do, with every able-bodied man in service or making armament?

"But there's something queer about him," he said. "And you may not know it, but we had a ship torpedoed out here last week. Some of the men landed on the beach. Some never landed anywhere, poor devils."

"I heard about it," said William. "What do you want me to do?"

"How the hell do I know?" said the Old Man. "Look around. See if there's anything suspicious. And if there isn't, get rid of him anyhow. I don't like him."

A thin flush rose to William's wrinkled face. "You mean I'm to stay?" he inquired.

"Why the devil do you suppose I brought you back?" shouted the Old Man. "Don't stand there staring. Get busy. We haven't got all night."

William's strictly amateur activities, however, yielded him nothing. His old room — now belonging to Jarvis — surprised him by its neatness, but unless that in itself was suspicious, there was nothing more. No flashlight for signaling, no code book, which William would certainly not have recognized anyhow, not even a radio.

"Tidy, is it?" said the Old Man when he reported back. "Well, I suppose that's that. I'd hoped to hand the F. B. I. a Christmas gift, but— All right, no spy. I've got another job for you, one you'll like better." He leaned back in his chair and eyed William quizzically. "Sally's not having a tree this year for the boy. I don't blame her. For months she's worked her fool head off. Army, Navy, and what have you. She's tired. Maybe she's breaking her heart. Sometimes I think she is. But by the Lord Harry he's having a tree just the same."

William looked at his watch.

"It's pretty late to buy one," he said. "But of course I can try."

The Old Man grinned, showing a perfect set of his own teeth, only slightly yellowed.

"Think I'm getting old, don't you?" he scoffed. "Always did think you were smarter than I was, didn't you? Well, I'm not in my dotage yet. The tree's on the porch. Had it delivered tonight. Unless," he added unkindly, "you're too feeble to drag it in!"

William also grinned, showing a perfect set of teeth, certainly not his own, except by purchase.

"I suppose you wouldn't care to take a bet on it, sir?" he said happily.

Ten minutes later the tree was in place in a corner of the Old Man's sitting room. William was perspiring but triumphant. The Old Man himself was exhilarated with one small drink and an enormous pride. Indeed, both were eminently cheerful until, without warning, they heard the sound of a car outside.

It was Sally, and before she had put up her car and got back to the house, William was hidden in the darkened sitting room, and her grandfather was sedately reading in his chair beside a lamp. From where he stood William could see her plainly. She had changed, he thought. She looked older. But she looked gentler, too, as though at last she had learned some of the lessons of life. Her eyes were no longer bleak, but they were sunken in her head. Nevertheless William felt a thrill of pride. She was their girl, his and the Old Man's, and now she was a woman. A lovely woman, too. Even William, no connoisseur, could see that.

"Good gracious, why aren't you in bed?" she said, slipping off her fur coat. "And where's the nurse?"

"It's Christmas Eve, my dear. I sent her off for a while. She'll be back."

But Sally was not listening. Even William could see that. She sat down on the edge of a chair and twisted her fingers in her lap.

"There wasn't any mail, was there?"

"I'm afraid not. Of course we don't know where he is. It may be difficult for him to send any."

Suddenly she burst out.

"Why don't you say it?" she demanded. "You always say what you think. I sent Tony off wrong. I can't forgive myself for that. I was wrong about William, too. You miss him, don't you?"

"Miss him?" said the Old Man, deliberately raising his voice. "Why would I miss the old rascal? Always pottering around and doing nothing! I get along fine without him."

"I think you're lying to make me feel better," she said, and got up. "I was wrong about him, and tonight I realized I'd been wrong about the baby's tree. When I saw the men around the one we'd fixed for them — I've made a mess of everything, haven't I?"

"Most of us do, my dear," said her grandfather. "But we learn. We learn."

She went out then, closing the door quietly behind her. When William went into the bedroom he found the Old Man staring somberly at the fire.

"Damn war anyhow," he said violently. "Damn

232

the blasted lunatics who wished it on the earth. All I need now is for some idiots to come around and sing 'Peace on earth, good will to men!' "

As though it might have been a signal, from beyond the window suddenly came a chorus of young voices, and William gingerly raised the shade. Outside, holding umbrellas in one hand and clutching their blowing cassocks around them with the other, the choir boys from the nearby church were singing, their small scrubbed faces earnest and intent. They sang about peace, and the King of peace who had been born to save the world, and the Old Man listened. When they had gone he grinned sheepishly.

"Well, maybe they're right at that," he said. "Sooner or later peace has to come. How about a small drink to the idea, anyhow?"

They drank it together and in silence, and once more they were back where they had been a year ago. No longer master and man, but two friends of long standing, content merely to be together.

"So you've been doing fine without me, sir?" said William, putting down his glass.

"Hell, did you hear that?" said the Old Man innocently.

They chuckled as at some ancient joke.

It was after eleven when William in his socks made his way to the attic where the trimmings for the tree were stored. Sally was still awake. He could hear her stirring in her room. For a moment he stood outside and listened, and it seemed no time at all since he had done the same thing when she was a child, and had been punished and sent to bed. He would stand at her door and tap, and she would open it and throw herself sobbing into his arms.

"I've been a bad girl, William."

He would hold her and pat her thin little back.

"Now, now," he would say. "Take it easy, Sally. Maybe William can fix it for you."

But of course there was nothing he could fix now. He felt rather chilly as he climbed the attic stairs.

To his relief the attic was orderly. He turned on the light and moving cautiously went to the corner where the Christmas tree trimmings, neatly boxed and covered, had always stood. They were still there. He lifted them, one by one, and placed them behind him. Then he stiffened and stood staring.

Neatly installed behind where they had been was a small radio transmitter.

He knew it at once for what it was, and a slow flush of fury suffused his face as he knelt down to examine it.

"The spy!" he muttered thickly, "the dirty devil of a spy!"

So this was how it was done. This was how ships were being sunk at sea; the convoys assembling, the ships passing along the horizon, and men like Jarvis watching, ready to unleash the waiting submarine wolves upon them.

He was trying to tear it out with his bare hands when he heard a voice behind him.

"Stay where you are, or I'll shoot."

But it was not Jarvis. It was Sally, white and terrified, in a dressing gown over her nightdress and clutching a revolver in her hand. William got up slowly and turned, and she gasped and dropped the gun.

"Why, William!" she said. "What are you doing here?"

He stood still, concealing the transmitter behind his stocky body.

"Your grandfather sent for me," he said, with dignity. "He was planning a little surprise for you and the boy, in the morning."

She looked at him, at his dependable old face, at the familiar celluloid collar gleaming in the light, at his independent sturdy figure, and suddenly her chin quivered.

"Oh, William," she said. "I've been such a dreadful person."

All at once she was in his arms, crying bitterly.

"Everything's so awful," she sobbed. "I'm so frightened, William. I can't help it."

And once more he was holding her and saying:

"It will be all right, Sally girl. Don't you worry. It will be all right."

She quieted, and at last he got her back to her room. He found that he was shaking, but he went methodically to work. He did what he could to put the transmitter out of business. Then he piled up the boxes of trimmings and carried them down the stairs. There was still no sign of Jarvis, and the Old Man was dozing in his chair. William hesitated. Then he shut himself in the sitting room and cautiously called the chief of the local police.

"This is William," he said. "The butler at Major Bennett's. I—"

"So you're back, you old buzzard, are you?" said the chief. "Well, Merry Christmas and welcome home."

But he sobered when William told him what he had discovered. He promised to round up some men, and not—at William's request—to come as if they were going to a fire.

"We'll get him all right," he said. "We'll get all these dirty polecats sooner or later. All right. No siren. We'll ring the doorbell."

William felt steadier after that. He was in the basement getting a ladder for trimming the tree when he heard Jarvis come back. But he went directly up the back stairs to his room, and

William, listening below, felt that he would not visit the attic that night.

He was singularly calm now. The Old Man was sound asleep by that time, and snoring as violently as he did everything else. William placed the ladder and hung the wax angel on the top of the tree. Then he stood precariously and surveyed it.

"Well, we're back," he said. "We're kind of old and battered, but we're still here, thank God."

Which in its way was a prayer too, like the Old Man's earlier in the evening.

He got down, his legs rather stiff, and going into the other room touched the sleeper lightly on the shoulder. He jerked awake.

"What the hell did you do that for?" he roared. "Can't a man take a nap without your infernal interfering?"

"The tree's ready to trim," said William quietly.

Fifteen minutes later the nurse came back. The bedroom was empty, and in the sitting room before a half-trimmed tree the Old Man was holding a small—a very small—drink in his hand. He waved his glass at her outraged face.

"Merry Christmas," he said, a slight—a very slight—thickness in his voice. "And get me that telegram that came for Sally today."

She looked disapprovingly at William, a William on whom the full impact of the situation—plus a very small drink—had suddenly descended like the impact of a pile-driver. Her austere face softened.

"You look tired," she said. "You'd better sit down."

"Tired? Him?" scoffed the Old Man. "You don't know him. And where the hell's that telegram?"

She brought it, and he put on his spectacles to read it.

"Sally doesn't know about it," he explained. "Held it out on her. Do her good." Then he read it aloud. "Home for breakfast tomorrow. Well. Love. Merry Christmas. Tony."

He folded it and looked around, beaming.

"How's that for a surprise?" he demanded. "Merry Christmas! Hell, it will be a real Christmas for everybody."

William stood still. He wanted to say something, but his voice stuck in his throat. Then he stiffened. Back in the pantry the doorbell was ringing.

The Lipstick

The Lipstick

I walked home after the coronor's inquest.
Mother had gone on in the car, looking rather
sick, as indeed she had done ever since Elinor's
death. Not that she had particularly cared for
Elinor. She has a pattern of life which divides
people into conformers and non-conformers. The
conformers pay their bills the first of the month,
go to church — the Episcopal, of course, never by
any chance get into anything but the society
columns of the newspapers, and regard marriage
as the *sine qua non* of every female over twenty.

My cousin Elinor Hammond had openly
flouted all this. She had gone gaily through life,
as if she wakened each morning wondering what
would be the most fun that day; stretching her
long lovely body between her silk sheets — how
mother resented those sheets! — and calling to
poor tired old Fred in his dressing room.

"Let's have some people in for cocktails,
Fred."

"Anything you say, darling."

It was always like that. Anything Elinor said was all right with Fred. He worshipped her. As I walked home that day I was remembering his face at the inquest. He had looked dazed.

"You know of no reason why your—why Mrs. Hammond should take her own life?"

"None whatever."

"There was nothing in her state of health to have caused her anxiety?"

"Nothing. She had always seemed to be in perfect health."

"She was consulting Doctor Barclay."

"She was tired. She was doing too much," he said unhappily.

Yet there it was. Elinor had either fallen or jumped from that tenth floor window of Doctor Barclay's waiting room, and the coroner plainly believed she had jumped. The doctor had not seen her at all that day. Only the nurse.

"There was no one else in the reception room," she testified. "The doctor was busy with a patient. Mrs. Hammond sat down by the window and took off her hat. Then she lit a cigarette and picked up a magazine. After that I went back to my office to copy some records. I didn't see her again until—"

She was a pretty little thing. She looked pale.

"Tell us what happened next," said the coroner gently.

"I heard the other patient leave about five

242

minutes later. She went out from the consulting room. There's a door there into the hall. We have that arrangement, so—well, so that patients don't meet. When he buzzed for the next case, I went in to get Mrs. Hammond. She wasn't there. I saw her hat, but her bag was gone. I thought she had gone to the lavatory. Then—" She stopped and gulped. "Then I heard people shouting in the street and I looked out the window."

The coroner gave her a little time. She got out a handkerchief and dabbed at her eyes.

"What would you say was her mental condition that morning, Miss Comings? Was she depressed?"

"I thought she seemed very cheerful," she said.

"The window was open beside her?"

"Yes. I couldn't believe it until I—"

He excused her then. She was openly crying by that time, and it was clear that she had told all she knew.

When Doctor Barclay was called—he had come in late—I was surprised. I had expected an elderly man, but he was only in the late thirties and quite good-looking. Knowing Elinor, I wondered. She had had a passion for handsome men, except for Fred, who had no looks whatever. Beside me I heard mother give a ladylike snort.

"So that's it!" she said. "She had as much need for a psychiatrist as I need a third leg."

But the doctor added little to what we already knew. He had not seen Elinor at all that morning. When he rang the buzzer and nobody came he had gone forward to the reception room. Miss Comings was leaning out the window. All at once she began to scream. Fortunately a Mrs. Thompson arrived at that time and took charge of her. He had gone down to the street, but the ambulance had already arrived.

He was frank enough up to that time. Queried about the reason for Elinor's consulting him he tightened, however.

"I have many patients like Mrs. Hammond," he said. "Women who live on their nerves. Mrs. Hammond had been doing that for years."

"That is all? She mentioned no particular trouble?"

He smiled faintly.

"We all have troubles," he said. "Some we imagine, some we magnify, some are real. But I would say that Mrs. Hammond was an unusually normal person. I had recommended that she go away for a rest. I believe she meant to do so."

His voice was clipped and professional. If Elinor had been attracted to him it had been apparently a one-sided affair. Fred, however, was watching him intently.

"You did not gather that she contemplated suicide?"

"No. Not at any time."

That is all they got out of him. He evaded them on anything Elinor had imagined, or magnified. In fact he did as fine a piece of dodging as I have ever seen. His relations with his patients, he said, were particularly confidential. If he knew anything of value he would tell it, but he did not.

Mother nudged me as he finished.

"Probably in love with her," she said. "He's had a shock. That's certain."

He sat down near us, and I watched him. I saw him reach for a cigarette, then abandon the idea, and I saw him more or less come to attention when the next witness was called. It was the Mrs. Thompson who had looked after the nurse, and she was a strangely incongruous figure in that group of Elinor's family and friends. She was a large motherly-looking woman, perspiring freely and fanning herself with a small folding fan.

She stated at once that she was not a patient.

"I clean his apartment for him once a week," she said. "He has a Jap, but he's no cleaner. That day I needed a little money in advance, so I went to see him."

She had not entered the office at once. She had looked in and seen Elinor, so she had waited in the hall, where there was a breeze. She had seen the last patient, a woman, leave by the consulting room door and go down in the elevator. A minute or so later she heard the nurse scream.

"She was leaning out the window yelling her head off," she said. "Then the doctor ran in and we got her on a couch. She said somebody had fallen out, but she didn't say who it was."

Asked how long she had been in the hall, she thought about a quarter of an hour. She was certain no other patient had entered during that time. She would have seen them if they had.

"You are certain of that?"

"Well, I was waiting my chance to see the doctor. I was watching pretty close. And I was never more than a few feet from the door."

"You found something belonging to Mrs. Hammond, didn't you? In the office?"

"Yes, sir. I found her bag."

The bag, it seemed, had been behind the radiator in front of the window.

"I thought myself it was a queer place for it, if she was going to—do what she did." And she added, naively, "I gave it to the police when they came."

So that was that. Elinor, having put her hat on the table, had dropped her bag behind the radiator before she jumped. Somehow it didn't make sense to me, and later on, of course, it made no sense at all.

The verdict was of suicide while of unsound mind. The window had been examined, but there was the radiator in front of it, and the general opinion seemed to be that a fall would have to be ruled out. Nobody of course mentioned murder. In the face of Mrs. Thompson's testimony it looked impossible. Fred listened to the verdict with blank eyes. His sister Margaret, sitting beside him and dressed in heavy mourning, picked up her bag and rose. And Doctor Barclay stared straight ahead of him as though he did not hear it. Then he got up and went out, and while I put mother in the car I saw him driving away, still with that queer fixed look on his face.

I was in a fine state of fury as I walked home. I had always liked Elinor, even when as mother rather inelegantly said, she had snatched Fred from under my nose. As a matter of cold fact, Fred Hammond never saw me after he first met her. He had worshipped her from the start, and his white, stunned face at the inquest only added to the mystery.

The fools, I thought. As though Elinor would ever have jumped out that window. Even if she was in trouble she would never have done it that way. There were so many less horrible ways. Sleeping tablets, or Fred's automatic, or even her smart new car and carbon-monoxide gas. But I refused to believe that she had done it at all. She had never cared what people thought. I remembered almost the last time I had seen her. Somebody had given a suppressed desire party, and

Elinor had gone with a huge red letter "A" on the front of her white satin dress.

Mother nearly had a fit when she saw it.

"I trust, Elinor," she said, "that your scarlet letter does not mean what it appears to mean."

Elinor had laughed.

"What do you think, Aunt Emma?" she said. "Would you swear that never in your life—"

"That will do, Elinor," mother said. "Only I am glad my dear sister is not alive, to see you."

She had been very gay that night, and she had enjoyed the little run-in with mother. Perhaps that was one of the reasons I had liked her. She could cope with mother. She could, of course. She wasn't an only daughter, living at home and on an allowance which was threatened every now and then. And she had brought laughter and gaiety into my own small world. Even her flirtations—and she was too lovely not to have plenty of them—had been lighthearted affairs, although mother had never believed it.

She was having tea when I got home. She sat stiffly behind the tea-tray and inspected me.

"I can't see why you worry about all this, Louise. You look dreadful," she said. "What's done is done. After all, she led Fred a miserable life."

"She made him happy, and now she's dead," I said shortly. "Also I don't believe she threw herself out that window."

248

"Then she fell."

"I don't believe that either," I said shortly.

"Nonsense! What do you believe?"

But I had had enough. I left her there and went upstairs to my room. It wasn't necessary for mother to tell me that I looked like something any decent dog would have buried. I could see that for myself. I sat down at my toilet table and rubbed some cream into my face, but my mind was running in circles. Somebody had killed Elinor and had gotten away with it. Yet who could have hated her enough for that? A jealous wife? It was possible. She had a way of taking a woman's husband and playing around with him until she tired of him. But she had not been doing that lately. She had been, for her, rather quiet.

Plenty of people of course had not liked her. She had a way of riding roughshod over them, ignoring their most sensitive feelings or laughing at them. She never snubbed anyone. She said what she had to say, and sometimes it wasn't pleasant. Even to Fred. But he had never resented it. He was like that.

I could see the Hammond place from my window, and the thought of Fred sitting there alone was more than I could bear. Not that I had ever been in love with him, in spite of mother's hopes. I dressed and went down to dinner, but I was still out of favor. I couldn't eat, either.

Luckily it was mother's bridge night, and after she and her three cronies were settled at the table I managed to slip out through the kitchen. Annie, the cook, was making sandwiches and cutting cake.

"It beats all, the way those old ladies can eat," she said resignedly.

I told her if I was asked for to say I had gone to bed, and went out. Fred's house was only two blocks away, set in its own grounds like ours, and as I entered the driveway I saw a man standing there, looking at it. I must have surprised him, for he turned suddenly and looked at me. It was Doctor Barclay.

He didn't recognize me, however. I suppose he had not even seen me at the inquest. He touched his hat and went out to the street, and a moment later I herd his car start off. But if he had been in the house Fred did not mention it. I rang and he himself opened the door. He seemed relieved when he saw me.

"I thought you were the damned police again," he said. "Come in. I've sent the servants to bed. They're all pretty well shot."

We went into the library. It looked as if it hadn't been dusted for a month. Elinor's house had always looked that way; full of people and cigarette smoke and used highball glasses. But at least it had looked alive. Now—well, now it didn't. So it was a surprise to see her bag lying on the table. Fred saw me looking it.

"Police returned it today," he said. "Want a drink?"

"I'll have some White Rock. May I look inside, it, Fred?"

"Go to it," he said dully. "There's nothing there that doesn't belong. No note, if that's what you mean."

I opened the bag. It was crammed as usual: compact, rouge, coin purse, a zipper compartment with some bills in it, a small memorandum book, a handkerchief smeared with lipstick, a tiny perfume vial, and some samples of dress material with a card pinned to them, "Match slippers to these." Fred was watching me over his glass, his eyes red and sunken.

"I told you. Nothing."

I searched the bag again, but I could not find the one thing which should have been there. I closed the bag and put it back on the table. But he wasn't paying any attention to me anyhow. He was staring at a photograph of Elinor in a silver frame, on the desk.

"All this police stuff," he said. "Why can't they just let her rest? She's asleep now, and she never got enough sleep. She was beautiful, wasn't she, Lou?"

"She was indeed," I said honestly.

"People said things. Margaret thought she was foolish and extravagant." He glanced at the desk

251

in the corner, piled high with what looked alike unopened bills. "Maybe she was, but what the hell did I care?"

He seemed to expect some comment, watching me out of haggard eyes. So I said:

"You didn't have to buy her, Fred. You had her. She was devoted to you."

He gave me a faint smile, like a frightened small boy who had been reassured.

"She was, you know, Lou," he said. "I wasn't only her husband. I was her father too. She told me everything. Why she had to go to that damned doctor—"

"Didn't you know she was going, Fred?"

"Not until I found a bill from him," he said grimly. "I told her I could prescribe a rest for her, instead of her sitting for hours with that young puppy. But she only laughed."

He talked on, as if he was glad of an audience. He had made her happy. She went her own way sometimes, but she always came back to him. He considered the coroner's verdict an outrage. "She fell. She was always reckless about heights." And he had made no plans, except that Margaret was coming to stay until he closed the place. And as if the mere mention of her had summoned her, at that minute Margaret walked in.

I had never liked Margaret Hammond. She was a tall angular woman, older than Fred, and she merely nodded to me.

"I decided to come tonight," she said. "I don't like your being alone. And tomorrow I want to inventory the house. I'd like to have father's portrait, Fred."

He winced at that. There had been a long quarrel about old Joe Hammond's portrait ever since Fred's marriage. Not that Elinor had cared about it, but because Margaret had always wanted it she had held onto it. I looked at Margaret. Perhaps she was the nearest to a real enemy Elinor had ever had. She had hated the marriage, had resented Elinor's easy-going extravagant life. Even now she could not help looking at the desk, piled high with bills.

"I'd rather straighten that for you," she said. "We'll have to find out how you stand."

"I know how I stand."

He got up and they confronted each other, Fred with his back to the desk, as if even then he was protecting Elinor from Margaret's prying eyes.

She shrugged and let it go. Yet as I left the house I was fairly confident she would spend the night at that desk. Fred asleep, the exhausted sleep of fatigue and escape, and Margaret creeping down to the desk, perhaps finding that bill of Doctor Barclay's and showing it to him in the morning.

"So that's how she put in her time! And you

pay for it!"

It was warm that night. I walked slowly home, hoping the bridge game was not over. But it seemed my night for unexpected encounters, for I had gone nearly half the way when I realized I was being followed. That is, someone was walking softly behind me. I felt the hair rising on my scalp as I stopped and turned. But it was only a girl. When I stopped she stopped too. Then she came on, and spoke my name.

"You're Miss Baring, aren't you?"

"Yes. You scared me half to death."

"I'm sorry. I saw you coming out of the inquest today, and a reporter told me your name. You've been to the Hammonds', haven't you?"

"Yes. What about it?"

She seemed uncertain. She stood still, fiddling with her handbag. She was quite young, and definitely uneasy.

"Were you a friend of Mrs. Hammond's?" she inquired.

"She was my cousin. Why?"

She seemed to make a decision, although she took her time to do it. She opened her bag, got out a cigarette and lit it before she answered.

"Because I think she was pushed out that window," she said, defiantly. "I'm in an office across the street, and I was looking out. I didn't know who she was, of course."

"Do you mean that you saw it happen?" I said

incredulously.

"No. But I saw her at the window, just before it happened, and she was using a lipstick. When I looked out again she was—she was on the pavement." She shivered, and threw away the cigarette. "I don't think a woman would use a lipstick just before she was going to do a thing like that, do you?"

"No," I said. "How long was it between that and when you saw her, down below?"

"Hardly a minute."

"You're sure it was Mrs. Hammond?"

"Yes. She had on a green dress, and I had noticed her hair. She didn't have a hat on. I—well, I went back tonight to see it the lipstick was somewhere on the pavement. I couldn't find it. The street was crowded. Anyhow someone may have picked it up. It's three days ago. But I'm pretty sure she still had it when she fell."

That was what I had not told Fred, that Elinor's gold lipstick was missing from her bag.

I looked at my watch. It was only eleven o'clock, and mother was good for another hour.

"We might go and look again," I said. "Do you mind?"

She didn't mind. She was a quiet-spoken girl, certain that Elinor had not killed herself. But she didn't want her name used. In fact, she would not tell me her name.

"Just call me Smith," she said. "I don't want

255

any part of this. I've got a job to hold."

I never saw her again, and unless she reads this she will probably never know that she took the first step that solved the case. Because I found the lipstick that night. It was in the gutter, and a dozen cars must have run over it. It was crushed flat, but after I had wiped the mud of Elinor's monogram was perfectly readable.

Miss Smith saw it and gasped.

"So I was right," she said.

The next minute she had hailed a bus and got on it, and as I say I have never seen her since.

I slept badly that night. I heard the party below breaking up and the cars driving away. When mother came upstairs she opened my door, but I turned off the light and closed my eyes, which was the only escape I knew of. I knew then that I had a murder to consider, and it seemed unimportant whether she had won two dollars or lost it that evening. But I got up after she had settled down for the night, and hid that battered lipstick in the lining of my hatbox.

It was late when I got to Doctor Barclay's office the next morning. The reception room door was unlocked and I walked in. The room was empty, so I went to the window and looked down. I tried to think that I was going to jump, and whether I would use a lipstick or not if I were. It only made me dizzy and weak in the knees, however, and when the nurse came in I felt like holding on to her.

If she recognized me she gave no sign of it.

"I don't think you have an appointment, have you?" she inquired.

"No, I'm sorry. Should I?"

She looked as though I had committed *lèse majesté*, no less; and when I gave my name she seemed even more suspicious. She agreed, however, to tell Doctor Barclay I was there, and after a short wait she took me back to the consulting room.

The doctor got up when he saw me, and I merely put Elinor's lipstick on the desk in front of him and sat down.

"I don't think I understand," he said, staring at it.

"Mrs. Hammond was at the window in your reception room, using that lipstick, only a minute before she fell."

"I see." He looked at it again. "I suppose you mean it fell with her."

"I mean that she never killed herself, doctor. Do you think a woman would rouge her mouth just before she meant to do—what we're supposed to think she did?"

He smiled, wryly.

"My dear girl," he said, "if you saw as much of human nature as I do that wouldn't surprise you."

"So Elinor Hammond jumped out your window with a lipstick in her hand, and you watch the Hammond house last night and then make a bolt for it when I appear. If that makes sense—"

It shocked him. He hadn't recognized me before. He leaned back in his chair and looked at me as if he was seeing me for the first time.

"I see," he said. "So it was you in the driveway."

"It was indeed."

He seemed to come to a decision then. He leaned forward in his chair.

"I suppose I'd better tell you, and trust you to keep it to yourself. I hadn't liked the way Mr. Hammond looked at the inquest. That sort of thing is my business. I was afraid he might— well, put a bullet through his head."

"You couldn't stop it, standing in the driveway," I said skeptically.

He laughed a little at that. It made him look less professional, more like a human being. Then he sobered.

"I see," he said. "Well, Miss Baring, whatever happened to Mrs. Hammond, I assure you I didn't do it. As for being outside the house, I've told you the truth. I was wondering how to get in when you came. His sister had called me up. She was worried."

"I wouldn't rely too much on what Margaret Hammond says. She hated Elinor like poison."

I got up on that and retrieved the lipstick. He

got up too, and surveyed me unsmilingly.

"You're a very young and attractive woman, Miss Baring. Why don't you let this drop? After all you can't bring her back. You know that."

"I know she never killed herself," I said stubbornly, and went out.

I was less surprised than I might have been to find Margaret in the reception room when I reached it. She was standing close to the open window from which Elinor had fallen, and for one awful minute I thought she was going to jump herself.

"Margaret!" I said sharply.

She jerked and turned. She never used makeup, and her face was a dead white. But I was surprised to find her looking absolutely terrified when she saw me. She pulled herself together, however.

"Oh, it's you, Louise," she said. "You frightened me." She sat down abruptly and wiped her face with her handkerchief. "She must have slipped, Lou. It would be easy. Try it yourself."

But I shook my head. I had no intention of leaning out that window. Not with Margaret behind me. She said she had come to pay Fred's bill for Elinor, and I let it go at that. Nevertheless there was something queer about her that day, and I felt shivery as I went down in the elevator. Women at her time of life sometimes go off-balance to the point of insanity.

I had some trouble in starting my car, which is how I happened to see her when she came out of the building. And then she did something that made me stop and watch her. There was no question about it. She was looking over the pavement and in the gutter. So she knew Elinor's lipstick had fallen with her. Either that or she had missed it out of the bag.

She didn't see me. She hailed a taxi and got into it, her tall figure in its deep mourning conspicuous in that summer crowd of thin light dresses. To this day I don't know why I followed her, except that she was sthe only suspect I had. Not that I really believed then that she had killed Elinor. All I knew was that someone had done it.

I did follow her, however. The taxi went on and on. I began to feel rather silly as it passed through the business section and into the residential part of town. Here the traffic was lighter and I had to fall back. But on thinly settled street the taxi stopped and Margaret got out. She did not see me or my car. She was looking at a frame house, set back from the street, and with a narrow porch in front of it, and as I watched her she climbed the steps and rang the bell.

She was there, inside the house, for almost an hour. I began to feel more idiotic than even. There were so many possible reasons for her being there; reasons which had nothing to do with Elinor. But when she finally came out I sat up in amazement.

The woman seeing her off on the porch was the Mrs. Thompson of the inquest.

I stooped to fix my shoe as the taxi passed me, but I don't believe Margaret even saw the car. Nor did Mrs. Thompson. She didn't go into the house at once. Instead she sat down on the porch and fanned herself with her apron, and she was still there when I went up the steps.

She looked surprised rather than apprehensive. I don't suppose she had seen me at the inquest. She didn't move.

"I hope you're not selling anything," she said, not unpleasantly. "If you are you needn't waste your time."

It was impossible to connect her with crime. Any crime. By the time a woman has reached fifty what she is is written indelibly on her. Not only on her face. On her hands, on the clothes she wears and the way she wears them. She was the sort who got up in the morning and cooked breakfast for a large family. Probably did her own washing, too. Her knuckles were large and the skin on them red, as if they were too much in hot water. But her eyes were shrewd as she surveyed me.

"I'm not selling anything." I said. "May I sit down and talk to you?"

261

"What about?" She was suspicious now. "I've got lunch to get. The children will be coming home from school."

She got up, and I saw I would have to be quick.

"It's about a murder," I said shortly. "There's such a thing as being accessory after the fact, and I think you know something you didn't tell at the Hammond inquest."

Her florid color faded somewhat.

"It wasn't a murder," she said. "The verdict—"

"I know all about that. Nevertheless I think it was a murder. What was Mrs. Hammond's sister-in-law doing here if it wasn't?"

She looked startled, but she recovered quickly.

"I never saw her before," she said. "She came to thank me for my testimony. Because it showed the poor thing did it herself."

"And to pay you for it, I suppose?"

She flushed angrily.

"Nobody paid me anything," she said. "And now I think you'd better go. If you think anybody can bribe me to lie you're wrong. That's all."

She went in and slammed the door, and I drove back to town, puzzled over the whole business. Was she telling the truth? Or had there been something she had not told at the inquest? Certainly I believed that the doctor had known more than he had told. But why conceal anything? I began to feel as though there was a sort of conspiracy around me, and it was rather frightening.

I was late for lunch that day, and mother was indignant.

"I can't imagine why, with nothing to do, you are always late for meals," she said.

"I've had plenty to do, mother," I told her. "I've been working on Elinor's murder."

She gave a small ladylike squeal.

"Murder?" she said. "Of course she wasn't murdered. Who would do such a thing?"

"Well, Margaret for one. She always loathed her."

"Women in Margaret's position in life do not commit crimes," she said pontifically. "Really I don't know what has happened to you, Louise. The idea of suspecting your friends —"

"She is no friend of mine. And Elinor was."

"So you'll stir up all sorts of scandal. Murder indeed! I warn you, Louise, if you keep on with this idiotic idea you will find yourself spread all over the newspapers. And I shall definitely stop your allowance."

With this dire threat she departed, and I spent the afternoon wondering what Doctor Barclay and the Thompson woman either knew or suspected, and in getting a shampoo and wave at Elinor's hairdresser's.

The girls there were more than willing to talk

about her, and the one who set my hair told me something I hadn't known.

"Here I was, waiting for her," she said. "And she was always so prompt. Of course she never came, and—"

"You mean you expected her here, the day it happened?"

"That's right," she agreed. "She had an appointment for four o'clock. When I got the paper on my way home I simply couldn't believe it. She'd always been so gay. Of course the last few weeks she hadn't been quite the same, but naturally I never dreamed—"

"How long since you noticed a change in her?" I asked.

"Well, let me see. About Easter, I think. I remember I liked a new hat she had, and she gave it to me then and there! Walked out in her bare head. I ran after her with it, but she wouldn't take it back. She said a funny thing, now I think of it. She said sometimes new hats were dangerous!"

I may have looked better when I left the shop, but what I call my mind was doing pinwheels. Why were new hats dangerous? And why had Elinor changed since Easter?

Fred had dinner with us that evening. At least he sat at the table and pushed his food around with a fork. Margaret hadn't come. He said she was in bed with a headache, and he spent most of the time talking about Elinor.

It was ghastly, of course. Even mother looked unhappy.

"I wish you'd eat something, Fred," she said. "Try to forget the whole thing. It doesn't do any good to go over and over it. You made her very happy. Always remember that."

Some time during the meal I asked him if anything had happened to upset Elinor in the spring. He stared at me.

"In the spring? When?"

"About Easter," I said. "I thought she'd been different after that. As if she wasn't well, or something."

"Easter?" he said. "I don't remember anything, Lou. Except that she started going to that damned psychiatrist about then."

"Why did she go to him, Fred?" mother inquired. "If she had any inhibitions I never noticed them."

If there was a barb in this he didn't notice it. He gave up all pretension of eating and lit a cigarette.

"You saw him," he said. "He is a good-looking devil. Maybe she liked to look at him. It would be a change from looking at me."

He went home soon after that. I thought, in spite of his previous protests, that he had resented the doctor's good looks and Elinor's visits to him. And I wondered if he was trying to build up a defense against her in his own mind; to remember her as less than perfect in order to ease his tragic sense of loss.

I slept badly. I kept seeing Fred's face, and so I was late for breakfast the next morning. Yes, we still go down to breakfast. Mother believes in the smiling morning face over the coffee cups, and the only reason I had once contemplated marrying Fred was to have a tray in bed. But at least she had finished the paper, and I took it.

Tucked away on a back page, only a paragraph or two, was an item reporting that Mrs. Thompson had been shot the night before!

I couldn't believe it.

I read and re-read it. She was not dead, but her condition was critical. All the police had been able to learn from the family was that she had been sitting alone on the front porch when it happened. Nobody had even heard the shot, or if they did they had thought it was the usual backfire. She had been found by her husband lying on the porch floor when he came home from a lodge meeting. That had been at eleven o'clock. She was unconscious when he found her, and the hospital reported her as being still too low to make a statement. She had been shot through the chest.

So she had known something, poor thing. Something that made her dangerous. And again I remembered Margaret, going up the steps of the little house on Charles Street. Margaret searching for Elinor's lipstick in the street, Margaret who had hated Elinor, and who was now in safe possession of Fred, of old Joe Hammond's portrait, of Elinor's silk sheets, and—I suddenly remembered—of Fred's automatic, which had lain in his desk drawer for years on end.

I think it was the automatic which finally decided me. That and Mrs. Thompson, hurt and perhaps dying. She had looked so—well, so motherly, sitting on that little porch of hers, with children's dresses drying on a line in the side yard, and her hands swollen with hard work. She had needed some money in advance, she had gone to the doctor's office to get it, and something had happened there that she either knew all the time, or had remembered later.

Anyhow I went to our local precinct stationhouse that afternoon, and asked a man behind a high desk to tell me who was in charge. He was eating an apple, and he kept on eating it.

"What's it about?" he said, eying me indifferently.

"It's a private matter."

"He's busy."

"All right," I said. "If he's too busy to look into a murder, then I'll go downtown to Headquarters."

He looked only mildly interested.

"Who's been murdered?"

"I'll tell *him* that."

There was an officer passing, and he called him.

"Young lady here's got a murder on her mind," he said. "Might see if the captain's busy."

The captain was not busy, but he wasn't interested either. When I told him it was about Elinor Hammond, he said he understood the case was closed, and anyhow it hadn't happened in his district. As Mrs. Thompson was not in his district either, and as he plainly thought I was either out of my mind or looking for publicity, I finally gave up. The man behind the desk grinned at me when I passed him on the way out.

"Want us to call for the corpse?" he inquired.

"I wouldn't ask you to call for a dead dog," I told him bitterly.

But there was a result, after all. I drove around the rest of the afternoon, trying to decide what to do. When I got home I found mother in the hall, looking completely outraged.

"There's a policeman here to see you," she hissed. "What on earth have you done?"

"Where is he?"

"In the living room."

"I want to see him alone, mother," I said. "I haven't done anything. It's about Elinor."

"I think you're crazy," she said furiously. "It's

all over. She got into trouble and killed herself. She was always headed for trouble. The first thing you know you'll be arrested yourself."

I couldn't keep her out. She followed me into the room, and before I could speak to the detective there she told him I had been acting strangely for the past few days, and that she was going to call a doctor and put me to bed. He smiled at that. He was a capable looking man, and he more or less brushed her off.

"Suppose we let her talk for herself," he said. "She looks quite able to. Now, Miss Baring, what's all this about a murder?"

So I told him, with mother breaking in every now and then to protest; about Elinor and the lipstick, about her appointment at her hairdresser's shortly after the time she was lying dead on the pavement, and my own conviction that Mrs. Thompson knew something she hadn't told.

"I gather you think Mrs. Hammond didn't kill herself. Is that it?"

"Does it look like it?" I demanded.

"Then who did it?"

"I think it was her sister-in-law."

Mother almost had a fit at that. She got up, saying she had heard enough nonsense, and that I was hysterical. But the detective did not move.

"Let her alone," he said gruffly. "What about this sister-in-law?"

"I found her in Doctor Barclay's office yesterday," I said. "She insisted that Elinor had fallen out the window. She said the floor was slippery, and she wanted me to try it myself." I lit a cigarette, and found to my surprise that my hands were shaking. "Maybe it sounds silly, but she knew about the lipstick. She tried to find it in the street."

But it was my next statement which really made him sit up.

"I think she was in the office the day Elinor was killed," I said. "I think the Thompson woman knew it. And I think she went out there last night and shot her."

"Shot her?" he said sharply. "Is that the woman out on Charles Street? In the hospital now?"

"Yes."

He eyed me steadily.

"Why do you think Miss Hammond shot her?" he said. "After all that's a pretty broad statement."

"Because she went there yesterday morning to talk to her. She was there an hour. I know. I followed her."

Mother started again. She couldn't imagine my behavior. I had been carefully reared. She had done her best by me. And as for Margaret, she had been in bed last night with a headache. It would be easy to verify that. The servants—

He waited patiently, and then got up. His face was expressionless.

"I have a little advice for you, Miss Baring," he said. "Leave this to us. If you're right and there's been a murder and a try at another one, that's our job. If you're wrong no harm's been done. Not yet, anyhow."

It was mother who went to bed that afternoon, while I waited at the telephone. And when he finally called me the news left me exactly where I had been before. Mrs. Thompson had recovered consciousness and made a statement. She did not know who shot her, or why, but she insisted that Margaret had visited her merely to thank her for her testimony, which had shown definitely that Elinor had either fallen or jumped out of the window. She had neither been given nor offered any money.

There was more to it, however. It appeared that Mrs. Thompson had been worried since the inquest and had called Margaret on the telephone to ask her if it was important. As a matter of fact, someone *had* entered the doctor's office while she was in the hall.

"But it was natural enough," he said. "It was the one individual nobody ever really notices. The postman."

"The postman?" I said weakly.

"Exactly. I've talked to him. He saw Mrs. Hammond in the office that morning. He remembers her all right. She had her hat off, and she was reading a magazine."

"Did he see Mrs. Thompson?"

"He didn't notice her, but she saw him all right."

"So he went out last night and shot her!"

He laughed.

"He took his family to the movies last night. And remember this, Miss Baring. That shot may have been an accident. Plenty of people are carrying guns now who never did before."

It was all very cheerio. Elinor had committed suicide and Mrs. Thompson had been shot by someone who was practising for Hitler. Only I just didn't believe it. I believed it even less after I had a visit from Doctor Barclay that night.

I had eaten dinner alone. Mother was still in bed refusing to see me, and I felt like an orphan. I was listening to the war news on the radio and wondering if I could learn enough about nursing to get away somewhere when the parlormaid showed him in. He was apparently not sure of his welcome, for he looked uncomfortable.

"I'm sorry to butt in like this," he said. "I won't take much of your time."

"Then it's not a professional call?"

He looked surprised.

"Certainly not. Why?"

"Because my mother thinks I'm losing my

272

mind," I said rather wildly. "Elinor Hammond is dead, so let her lie. Mrs. Thompson is shot, but why worry? Remember the papers! Remember the family name! No scandal, please. No—"

"See here," he said. "You're in pretty bad shape, aren't you? How about going to bed? I'll talk to you later."

"So I'm to go to bed!" I said nastily. "That would be nice and easy, wouldn't it? Somebody is getting away with murder. Maybe two murders. And everybody tries to hush me up. Even the police!"

That jolted him.

"You've been to police?"

"Why not? Why shouldn't the police be told? Just because you don't want it known that someone was pushed out of your office window—"

He was angry. He hadn't sat down, and I made no move to do so. We must have looked like a pair of chickens with our feathers spread ready to fight. But he tried to control himself.

"See here," he said. "You're dealing with things you don't understand. Good God, why can't you stay out of this case?"

"There wasn't any case until I made one," I said furiously. "I don't understand. Why is everybody warning me off?" I suppose I lost control then. The very way he was watching me set me off. "How do I know you didn't do it yourself? You could have. Either you or the postman.

273

And he was at the movies!"

"The postman!" he said staring. "What do you mean, the postman?"

I suppose it was his astonished face which made me laugh. I laughed and laughed. I couldn't stop. Then I was crying too. I couldn't stop that either. I could hear myself practically screaming, and suddenly and without warning he slapped me in the face.

It jerked my head back and he had to catch me. But it stopped me all right. I pulled loose from him and told him to get out of the house. He didn't move, however. It didn't help to see that he had stopped looking angry; that in fact he seemed rather pleased with himself.

"That's the girl," he said. "You'd have had the neighbors in in another minute. You'd better go up to bed, and I'll send you some sleeping stuff from the drugstore."

"I wouldn't take anything you sent me on a bet," I said bitterly.

He ignored that. He redeemed my cigarette from where it was busily burning a hole in the carpet—good heavens! Mother!—and dropped it in an ash tray. Then to my fury he leaned down and patted me on the shoulder.

"Believe it or not," he said. "I didn't come here to attack you! I came to ask you not to go out alone at night, until I tell you you may." He picked up his hat. "I mean what I'm saying," he added. "Don't go out of this house alone at night, Miss Baring. Any night."

"Don't be ridiculous," I said, still raging. "Why shouldn't I go out at night?"

He was liking me less and less by the minute. I could see that.

"Because it may be dangerous," he said shortly. "And I particularly want you to keep away from the Hammond house, I mean that, and I hope you'll have sense enough to do it."

He banged the front door when he went out, and I spent the next half hour trying to smooth the burned spot in the carpet and hating him like poison. I was still angry when the telephone rang in the hall. It was Margaret!

"I suppose we have you to thank for the police coming here tonight," she said. "Why in heaven's name can't you leave us alone? We're in trouble enough, without you making things worse."

"All right," I said recklessly. "Now I'll ask you one. Why did you visit Mrs. Thompson yesterday morning? And who shot her last night?"

She did not reply. She gave a sort of gasp. Then she hung up the receiver.

It was a half hour later when the druggist's boy brought the sleeping tablets. I took them back to the kitchen and dropped them in the coal range, while Annie watched me with amazement. She was fixing mother's hot milk, I remember, and she told me that Clara, the

Hammonds' cook, had been over that night.

"She says things are queer over there," she reported. "Somebody started the furnace last night, and the house was so hot this morning you couldn't live in it."

I didn't pay much attention. I was still pretty much shaken. Then I saw Annie look up, and Fred was standing on the kitchen porch, smiling his tired apologetic smile.

"May I come in?" he said. "I was taking a walk and I saw the light."

He looked better, I thought. He said Margaret was in bed, and the house was lonely. Then he asked if Annie would make him a cup of coffee.

"I don't sleep much anyhow," he said. "It's hard to get adjusted. And the house is hot. I've been getting rid of a lot of stuff. Burning it."

So that explained the furnace. I hoped Annie heard it.

I walked out with him when he left, and watched him as he started home. Then I turned up the driveway again. I was near the house when it happened. I remember the shrubbery rustling, and stopping to see what was doing it. But I never heard the shot. Something hit me on the head. I fell, and after that there was a complete blackout until I heard mother's voice. I was in my own bed, with a bandage around my head and an ache in it that made me dizzy.

"I warned her," mother was saying, in a strangled tone. "The very idea of going out when you told her not to!"

"I did my best," said a masculine voice. "But you have a very stubborn daughter, Mrs. Baring."

It was Doctor Barclay. He was standing beside the bed when I opened my eyes. I suppose I was still confused, for I remember saying feebly:

"You slapped me."

"And a lot of good it did," he retorted briskly. "Now look where you are! And you're lucky to be there."

I could see him better by that time. He looked very queer. One of his eyes was almost shut, and his collar was a wilted mess around his neck. I stared at him.

"What happened?" I asked dizzily. "You've been in a fight."

"More or less."

"And what's this thing on my head?"

"That," he said, "is what you get for disobeying orders."

I began to remember then, the scuffling in the bushes, and something knocking me down. He reached over calmly and took my pulse.

"You've got a very pretty bullet graze on the side of your head," he said calmly. "Also I've had to shave off quite a bit of your hair." I suppose I wailed at that, for he shifted from my pulse to my hand. "Don't worry about that," he said. "It was very pretty hair, but it will grow again. At least thank God you're here!"

"Who did it? Who shot at me?"

"The postman, of course," he said, and to my rage and fury went out of the room.

I slept after that. I suppose he had given me something. Anyhow it was the next morning before I heard the rest of the story. Mother had fallen for him completely, and she wouldn't let him see me until my best silk blanket cover was on the bed, and I was surrounded by baby pillows. Even then in a hand mirror I looked dreadful, with my head bandaged and my skin a sort of yellowish gray. He didn't seem to mind, however. He came in, big and smiling, with his right eye purple and completely closed by that time and told me I looked like the wrath of heaven.

"You're not looking your best yourself," I said.

"Oh, that!" he observed, touching his eye gingerly. "Your mother put a silver knife smeared with butter on it last night. Quite a person, mother. We get along fine,"

He said I was to excuse his appearance, because he hadn't been home. He had been busy all night with the police. He thought he would go there now and clean up. And with that my patience gave way completely.

"You're not moving out of this room until I

278

know what's been going on," I stormed. "I'm running a fever right now, out of pure excitement."

He put a big hand on my forehead.

"No fever," he said. "Just your detective mind running in circles. All right. Where do I start?"

"With the postman."

So then he told me. Along in the spring Elinor had come to him with a queer story. She said she was being followed. It made her nervous. In fact, she was pretty well frightened. It seemed that the man who was watching her wherever she went wore a postman's uniform. She would be having lunch at a restaurant — perhaps with what she called a man friend — and he would be outside a window. He would turn up in all sorts of places. Of course it sounded fantastic, but she swore it was true.

Some faint ray of intelligence came to me.

"Do you mean it was this man the Thompson woman remembered she had seen going into your office?"

"She's already identified him. The real letter carrier had been there earlier. He had seen Mrs. Hammond sitting in a chair, reading a magazine. But he had gone before the Thompson woman arrived. The one she saw was the one who — well, the one who killed Elinor."

I think I knew before he told me. I know I felt sick.

"It was Fred, wasn't it?"

"It was Fred Hammond. Yes." He reached over and took my hand. "Tough luck, my dear," he said. "I was worried about it. I tried to get her to go away, but you knew her. She wouldn't do it. And then not long ago she wore a dress at a party with the scarlet letter 'A' on it, and I suppose that finished him."

"It's crazy," I gasped. "He adored her."

"He had an obsession about her. He loved her, yes. But he was afraid he might lose her. Was losing her. And he was wildly jealous of her." He looked slightly embarrassed. "I think now he was particularly jealous of me."

"But if he really loved her—"

"The line between love and hate is pretty fine. And it's just possible too that he felt she was never really his until—well, until no one else could have her."

"So he killed her!"

"He killed her," he said slowly, "He knew that nobody notices the postman, so he walked into my office and—"

He got up and went to the window. I sat up dizzily in bed.

"But he was insane," I said. "You can't send him to the chair."

"Nobody will send him to the chair," he said somberly. "Just remember this, my dear. He's better off where he is. Perhaps he has found his wife by this time. I think he hoped that." He hesitated. "I was too late last night. I caught him just in time when he fired at you, but he put up a real battle. He got loose somehow and shot himself."

He went on quietly. There was no question of Fred's guilt, he said. Mrs. Thompson in the hospital had identified his photograph as that of the postman she had seen going into the office, and coming out shortly before she heard the nurse screaming. The bullet with which she had been shot had come from Fred's gun. And Margaret— poor Margaret—had been suspicious of his sanity for a long time.

"She came to see me yesterday after she learned the Thompson woman had been shot. She wanted him committed to an institution, but she got hysterical when I mentioned the police. I suppose there wasn't much of a case, anyhow. With Mrs. Thompson apparently dying and the uniform gone—"

"Gone? Gone how?"

"He'd burned it in the furnace. We found some charred buttons and things last night."

I lay still, trying to think.

"Why did he try to kill Mrs. Thompson?" I asked. "What did she know?"

"She had not only remembered seeing a postman going in and out of my office just before Miss Comings screamed. She even described him. And Margaret went home and searched the house. She found the uniform in a trunk in the attic. She knew then.

"She collapsed, She couldn't face Fred. She locked herself in her room, trying to think what to do. But she had told Fred she was going to see Mrs. Thompson that day, and she thinks perhaps he knew she had found the uniform. Something might have been disturbed. She doesn't know, nor do I. All we do know is that he left this house that night, got out his car, and tried to kill the only witness against him. Except you, of course."

"Except me!" I said.

"Except you," he repeated drily. "I tried to warn you, you may remember! I came here and you threw me out."

"But why me? He had always like me. Why should he try to kill me?"

"Because you wouldn't leave things alone," he said. "Because you were a danger from the minute you insisted Elinor had been murdered. And because you telephoned Margaret last night and asked her why she had visited Mrs. Thompson, and who had shot her."

"You think he was listening in?"

· "I know he was listening in. He wasn't afraid of his sister. She would have died to protect him, and he knew it. But here you were, a child with a stick of dynamite, and you come out with a think like that! That was when Margaret sent me to warn you."

I suppose I flushed.

"I'm sorry," I said guiltily. "I've been a fool all along, of course."

His one remaining eye twinkled.

"I wouldn't go as far as that," he said. "That stubbornness of yours really broke the case. Not," he added, "that I like stubborn women. Gentle and mild is my motto."

I had no difficulty in getting him back to the night before. He seemed to want to forget it. But he finally admitted that he had been watching the Hammond house all evening, and that when Fred came to our kitchen door he had been just outside. Fred however had seemed quiet. He drank his coffee and lit a cigarette. And then of course I had walked out to the street with him.

"Good God," he said. "If ever I wanted to waylay anyone and beat her up—!"

However, it had looked all right at first. Fred had started down the street toward home, and he followed him behind the hedge. But just too late he lost him, and he knew he was on his way back. Fred had his revolver lifted to shoot me when he grabbed him.

Suddenly I found I was crying. It was all horrible. Elinor at the window, and Fred behind her. Mrs. Thompson, resting after a hard day's work, and Fred shooting her. And I myself—

He got out a grimy handkerchief and dried my eyes.

"Stop it," he said. "It's all over now, and you're a very plucky young woman, Louise Baring. Don't spoil the record."

He got up rather abruptly.

"I think you've had enough of murder and sudden death," he said lightly. "What you need is quiet. I'm giving up your case, you know. There will be someone in soon to dress that head of yours."

"Why can't you do it?"

"I'm not that sort of doctor."

I looked up at him. He was haggard and tight with strain. He was dirty, he needed a shave, and that awful eye of his was getting blacker by the minute. But he was big and strong and sane. A woman would be safe with him, I thought. Any woman. Although of course she could never tell him her dreams.

"I don't see why you can't look after me," I said. "If I'm to look bald I'd prefer you to see it. After all you did it."

He grinned. Then to my surprise he leaned down and kissed me lightly on the cheek.

"I've wanted to do that ever since you slammed that lipstick down in front of me," he said. "And now for God's sake will you stop being a detective and concentrate on growing some hair on the side of your head? Because I'm going to be right around for a considerable time."

When I looked up mother was in the doorway, beaming.

THE BESTSELLING NOVELS
BEHIND THE BLOCKBUSTER MOVIES —
ZEBRA'S MOVIE MYSTERY GREATS!

HIGH SIERRA   (2059, $3.50)
by W.R. Burnett
A dangerous criminal on the lam is trapped in a terrifying web of circumstance. The tension-packed novel that inspired the 1955 film classic starring Humphrey Bogart and directed by John Houston.

MR. ARKADIN   (2145, $3.50)
by Orson Welles
A playboy's search to uncover the secrets of financier Gregory Arkadin's hidden past exposes a worldwide intrigue of big money, corruption — and murder. Orson Welles's only novel, and the basis for the acclaimed film written by, directed by, and starring himself.

NOBODY LIVES FOREVER   (2217, $3.50)
by W.R. Burnett
Jim Farrar's con game backfires when his beautiful victim lures him into a dangerous deception that could only end in death. A 1946 cinema classic starring John Garfield and Geraldine Fitzgerald. (AVAILABLE IN FEBRUARY 1988)

BUILD MY GALLOWS HIGH   (2341, $3.50)
by Geoffrey Homes
When Red Bailey's former lover Mumsie McGonigle lured him from the Nevada hills back to the deadly hustle of New York City, the last thing the ex-detective expected was to be set up as a patsy and framed for a murder he didn't commit. The novel that inspired the screen gem OUT OF THE PAST, starring Robert Mitchum and Kirk Douglas. (AVAILABLE IN APRIL 1988)

Available wherever paperbacks are sold, or order direct from the Publisher. Send cover price plus 50¢ per copy for mailing and handling to Zebra Books, Dept. 2764, 475 Park Avenue South, New York, N.Y. 10016. Residents of New York, New Jersey and Pennsylvania must include sales tax. DO NOT SEND CASH.